CABIN 2

STEELE SHADOWS SECURITY

AMANDA MCKINNEY

HH TISEVICH

Paperback ISBN 978-1-7340133-2-0
eBook ISBN 978-1-7340133-0-6

Editor(s): Nancy Brown
Cover Design: Amanda Traylor

https://www.amandamckinneyauthor.com

DEDICATION

For Mama, the wind at my back. We're getting there. :)

ALSO BY AMANDA

And many more to come...

LET'S CONNECT!

Text AMANDABOOKS to 66866 to sign up
for Amanda's Newsletter and get the latest
on new releases, promos, and freebies!
Or, you can sign up below.

https://www.amandamckinneyauthor.com

CABIN 2

Hidden deep in the remote mountains of Berry Springs is a private security firm where some go to escape, and others find exactly what they've been looking for.

Welcome to Cabin 1, Cabin 2, Cabin 3...

Always be prepared, that was Axel Steele's motto. While his brothers were throwing down at the local bar, Ax was the guy in the background devising the getaway plan. Dubbed "the smart one," the former special-ops Marine believed in structure and routine, a way of life the universe seemed hell-bent on challenging. Amidst a firestorm of family drama, Ax finds a woman held captive in the middle of the woods, and in desperate need of his help. With an armful of tattoos as colorful as her attitude, his new client is his antithesis—a free-spirited, spontaneous hippie that tests every bit of his patience... and his self-restraint.

Erika Zajac has been living life on her own terms since she was just sixteen. But her gypsy lifestyle came to a screeching halt when the horrific past she'd tried so hard to bury came back in the form of chains and cuffs. Suddenly, Erika finds herself under the security—and scrutiny—of a temperamental bodyguard with the emotional capacity of a rock, and six-pack to match. But no amount of brains or brawn was going to distract her from her goal, or the secrets she'd kill to keep.

Deceit, lies, wrath. Ax's client had them all. The only question was, which of Erika's deadly sins would she choose? Revenge... or him?

1

ERIKA

*M*y lungs burned as I sprinted up the mountain, my pulse drowning out the thrum of bugs around me. A bead of sweat rolled down my face, followed by another. I didn't wipe it, I didn't care. Cross-training was not the place for babies. In fact, I kind of liked it because sweat was proof that I was pushing myself to the limits, and that's exactly what I intended to do. I'd been told it was the steepest mountain in the area. What I hadn't been told was that thing was almost vertical, and the "jogging trails" were nothing more than a rocky path cut out of dense forest. That was fine though. My quads were on fire, but that was fine, too. No gain without pain. An overused cliché, but it was true. I had to believe that something good came from pain. That *all* pain somehow had its purpose. Yin and yang. If only that saying were true for everything in life. If only *all* pain really did lead to gain.

Because I was a walking example that it didn't.

Another bead down my forehead, this one dripping off my nose. I let it go without swiping it, then let another one drip. Just let it go, I thought. As if the universe awarded me for my sweat-accepting badassery, a gust of wind swept past me, cooling my slicked skin. I breathed in the crisp air, the spicy scent of fall. I'd ditched my jacket somewhere along the trail mid-mountain. It pained me to toss the brand-new windbreaker, but I could always get another, more often than not, at no cost. A bonus to my fitness obsession was that I'd gotten to know the manager at the local athletic store personally, and in my bed. Free samples and stamina. Heck of a combination. Besides, if someone took the jacket it must be because they needed it. It was my gift to them. A good deed is never lost. Right, universe?

I ground my teeth and focused on the crest of the mountain where the trail evened out, then disappeared into the trees again.

Pat, pat, pat, my running shoes pounded the pine needles beneath me. My legs tingled with fatigue, a familiar feeling giving me that extra push to finish.

Screw you mountain, I repeated over and over, my heart feeling like it was about to explode in my chest. Another blast of wind, except this time it felt like I was running through a wall of water. I see you, universe, and I raise you. A blow of adrenaline had me pushing harder as the wind continued to challenge me, this time with a tornado of crisp orange and red leaves swirling around me. One pelted me directly in the forehead, hellbent on breaking my focus.

Bastard.

Beautiful bastard, but one nonetheless.

Come on, come on. Endorphins burst through my veins, carrying me up the last few yards until finally, I crested the top of the mountain.

I doubled over, chest heaving, and checked my watch.

Record broken.

I sputtered a maniacal sounding laugh and straightened. A trio of birds darted away in response.

I'd beaten my personal best and it felt good.

Damn. Good.

I'd been told The Red Rock trail was infamous for its steep climbs and brutal switchbacks—and today proved that to be true. A total of fifteen miles roundtrip through one of the most treacherous mountains in Berry Springs. Cliffs, valleys, caves, boulders, a new obstacle every turn, it seemed. And that was good, exactly what I needed, because the annual Hippie Harvest race was coming up in a few weeks and finishing second place again was as acceptable as a tattoo inked by a drunken artist. Trust me on that.

I put my hands on my hips and did a slow turn. The wind whistled through the trees above me, birds chattering, squirrels scurrying. The sound of nature, a stillness, a calmness that only Mother Nature could provide. My gaze landed on a glorious sugar maple tree, a shimmering gold under the late afternoon sun. I traced the glowing silhouette in my mind, like a brush on a canvas, taking note of the various shades, textures, each coming together in a brilliant display.

A crow called out, its haunting caw pulling my attention behind me.

I frowned, the high from my jog beginning to waver.

Where the heck was I?

Thirty minutes earlier, I'd decided it was a great idea to veer off the trail and blaze my own path up the mountain in an attempt to challenge myself. Nothing like un-manicured trails to kick the burn up a notch. The problem was, I hadn't marked my route.

I glanced up at the waning sun, hanging above a mountain peak in the distance. Dusk was approaching and I guessed I had about an hour of daylight left. Better get a move on. Although I wasn't sure where I was, I knew that *down* was the best way to find myself. After a few gulps of water, I started back down the mountain. Minutes passed as I focused on my steps against the dirt, suddenly aware of how alone I was. No voices, laughter, joggers, or hikers. No rumbles of engines, dirt bikes, giggling children, nothing.

The breeze had stilled, halted, along with every creature around me it seemed. No squirrels, birds.

Nothing.

I glanced over my shoulder, my stomach tickling with nerves. How had I ventured so far from the trail? As much as I'd like to say that it wasn't like me to be that irresponsible, making decisions without thinking them through was kind of my thing. I'd followed a whim; gone in the direction that I was pulled, as I always did. And that blessed spontaneity had gotten me lost... again. Spontaneity, or, reckless impulsion as my brother would call it.

My psychologist called it restlessness.

But a life filled with schedules, meetings, endless events, mindless small talk, shameless butt-kissing? That kind of lifestyle went to my brother. Spending days behind a computer, analyzing reports, drowning in unread emails? No. No, that wasn't me. I'd rather play the starring role in an eighties sex-ed film for high school students than spend my days behind glowing monitors.

Me? Eccentric, beatnik, flighty, flower child, and my personal favorite—Beverly Hills Boho. Those were a few of the names I'd been called, although I preferred free-spirit. I took life as it came, one day at a time, a notion that was nothing less than alien to my elitist upbringing.

One day at a time. I knew all too well that life was too short not to stop and smell the roses. A mantra I'd set in stone the day I turned sixteen, stole my father's credit card and caught the first flight to Europe with nothing but a carry on. A Louis Vuitton carry-on, but carry-on nonetheless. I'd made it through Greece, Bulgaria, and was on my way to Istanbul when I encountered a young, handsome, yet prickly-looking fellow sent by my father to pack me up and send me home. His latest and greatest Harvard educated intern, I'd learned. So, after a few nights showing him more than just the sights, I'd packed up and journeyed home, leaving Jake-the-intern heartbroken in the penthouse suit of the Royal Palace, and my mini-crisis in the rearview mirror. I'd arrived home to frozen credit cards and a note that told me to get a real job.

So, I'd traded the Cartier watch dear Daddy had gotten me for my thirteenth birthday for a rusted Volkswagen hatchback and crossed the border, earning me fluency in Spanish and a wicked case of food poisoning.

And I never took a single penny from him again. Not one single penny from the Zajac fortune.

Water off a duck's back, that was my motto.

That was my motto the day I'd challenged myself on Red Rock Trail.

That was my motto the day that unearthed a past I'd tried so desperately to forget.

Bracing myself on a sapling, I edged over a boulder, sliding on loose rocks. The terrain was becoming rockier, steeper, and I had no memory of the area. A tingle of fear, maybe more like awareness, slid up my spine. And looking back, that was the moment—the moment that I should have beelined it down the mountain without looking back. Trusted my instinct—that little warning bell.

Did I? Of course not.

I picked my way through the brush, shadows from the

slanting sun swaying back and forth in a breeze I didn't feel. The world was darkening around me, as if I needed anything else to add to the sudden creep-factor I was feeling.

Clank, clank, clank...

I froze, my ears perking at the pitched sound breaking the eerie silence of the woods.

Clank, clank, clank...

A tapping, in perfect repetition, somewhere in the distance.

Metal on metal.

What the heck was metal on metal in the middle of nowhere?

My wildest dreams, my most terrifying nightmares couldn't prepare me for what happened next.

Perhaps it was my naturally inquisitive side that, according to my dad I'd gotten from my mom, but, true to Erika Zajac form—and against all better judgement—I veered off course, again, and followed the noise.

Clank, clank, clank...

I came up on a small clearing, confident the banging was becoming louder, and more confident that it was coming from underground.

My pulse started to pick up as I stepped out of the cover of the tree line, exposing myself to whatever was triggering my sudden anxiety. I stood out in the open feeling like I was stark-raving naked at the Super Bowl. I looked around the circle of woods lining the clearing, darkening in the shadows.

Again, good time to turn around and go back.

Nope. Not me. Not this genius.

I forced one foot in front of the other, picking my way to the middle of the clearing.

Clank, clank, clank...

The incessant tapping now becoming one with my thudding heartbeat, I stepped up to a boulder, extended to tiptoes and peeked over, half expecting the headless horseman to jump out. Instead, what I got was the corner of a small trap door covered in dead leaves and twigs.

My eyes popped. A trap door in the middle of the woods?

Clank, clank...

The noise was coming from whatever was behind that door. Whatever the heck was locked deep underground.

I looked around again, pulling my cell phone from the pocket of my leggings.

No reception. Of course.

I focused back on the door, chewing a hole in the bottom of my lip.

Clank, clank...

Pushing the apprehension aside, because God knew I was good at that, I shoved my cell back into my pocket and scrambled over the rock. A thin beam of sunlight, I swear the last beam of the day, shone like a beacon onto the door. Like a magnet pulling me to it.

Okay, universe, I remember thinking as I swept away the debris revealing a metal lock—*new*. A brand-new metal lock on a rusty trap door deep in the mountains.

The clanking had stopped at this point, and I found myself desperate to hear it again for some odd reason. Desperate to ensure what it was, was okay.

Like it was my very own mission.

It was a key lock, not a combination. I'd picked a number of locks in my day, most notably when I'd forgotten my keys on my way for a night out. How could this be different? I huffed out a breath, and as if accepting the challenge

—and now wanting to know more than ever what was in there—I went in search for something to pick it.

Nine twigs, one narrow rock, and dusk officially settling into the woods later, the lock gave with a loud *pop*, second only to the skipping of my heart.

My hands were unsteady as I removed the shiny metal and set it aside.

It was then, I had a moment. *Stay or leave. Stay or leave, Erika.*

With a defiant inhale—because only crazy people listened to the voices in their heads—I grabbed the flat, thin handle and lifted the door. The musty scent of damp earth wafted into my face as I peered at the narrow, wooden ladder fading into a pitch-black hole in the ground.

The first thing I noticed was that the ladder also appeared to be new, and clean. That, along with the lock, confirmed my suspicions that despite the remote location of the place, someone was actively using it.

Or, hiding something in it.

I glanced over one shoulder, then the other, my mind racing.

I turned back to the hole, the clanking sound looping on repeat in my head as I contemplated what to do.

Taking a deep breath, I leaned in. *"Hello?"* I cringed at my voice echoing off the once quiet woods like a foghorn announcing my location. Announcing that I was snooping somewhere that, I knew, one-hundred percent, I shouldn't be.

No response from the pit.

I gripped the sides and stuck my head inside, and called out again. Still nothing.

With a clench of my jaw, I shuffled, lowered my legs into the hole and took the first step, then the next, then the next.

With each step, my pulse drummed, my knees *literally* shaking. Finally, my shoes hit dirt.

Standing in a dim pool of whatever daylight was left, I turned, blinking into the blackness that surrounded me.

You've probably heard the expression, *'I could feel someone staring at me.'* That moment, I knew without question, that someone was looking at me. Staring at me. The air around me was still, the room was silent, but there was no doubt in my mind that someone, something, was there with me.

A presence.

2

ERIKA

*D*arkness enveloped me like a thick cloak, draping over my face, my eyes, my body, stealing my sight, a sense I would never take for granted again. It was so dark that I could almost *feel* the blackness. A presence, neither dead nor alive, shifting around me. Taunting me. Like the devil himself, although now, I knew that the devil himself was very real, and walked among us.

The human mind is an incredible thing, but as equally deceptive. Good and evil. I'd seen evil up close and personal thirteen years earlier, and relived that moment every night in my nightmares since. But this, this was... different.

I flexed my wrists against the metal cuffs, flinching at the sharp pain of the open wounds from where I'd tried to slide out of them. Cuffs, secured at the end of a heavy metal chain anchored to the cold, wet stone wall. Another pair clamped my ankles, the chains not even long enough to stretch my legs or to stand. Even though I ached from being curled up for so long, the pains reminded me that I was still alive. That my body still worked, that I still felt.

That I was still human and not fading into some sort of

shadowed purgatory where I would remain for the rest of my existence.

That I wasn't going crazy.

Unlike the man who'd come down the ladder after me, and before I could even react, slammed the butt of a gun into the back of my head, sending me face-first into the dirt. I'd vomited on impact, earning a swift kick in the side.

No words were spoken, just quick shuffles mixed with wafts of air scented with cheap whiskey breath and sweat as I was ripped from my keys and cellphone and dragged across the floor in my dazed state, then chained to the wall.

I fought, though. With every bit of my strength, I fought.

I remember his arm sweeping past my breast as he chained me, and an ice-cold fear paralyzing me. I hadn't realized until that point that perhaps the guy wanted what most men wanted from a woman, or worse, maybe I was about to enter a sadistic sex slavery ring. I had no idea. All I knew was that one minute I was investigating a weird clanking sound, and then next I was passed out in the hole in the ground.

But he didn't notice my breasts, or he didn't care, I wasn't sure. After chaining my wrists and ankles, he'd left me there with a throbbing headache and aching side.

I'd craned my neck as he'd opened the trap door, hoping to see his face. No luck.

I'll never forget hearing that lock click into place, a punctuation of my capture. And when I heard his boots stomping away, I knew I was going to be down there awhile. So, that moment, using my fingernail, I made a small nick on my wrist.

Day 1.

God, the darkness.

That inky black.

One thing I learned was that darkness—*real* darkness—had a way of overcoming sanity.

It didn't take me long to discover, though, that while my vision was taken from me, my other senses seemed to heighten.

Believe me, I wish they hadn't.

Because the second I sniffed that gut-wrenching, metallic scent of blood, I *knew* I wasn't alone. That the clanking I'd followed into the hole and the presence I'd felt when I'd stepped off the ladder was coming from someone, *something.* And that someone, or something, was hurt. Badly. And it wasn't until I smelled the sour scent of body odor, and the musty scent of urine that I realized that they'd been there a lot longer than I.

I'd waited hours—*hours*—before getting the courage to say something. Correction, whisper something.

"Hello," I'd finally said in a voice barely detectable to the human ear, while my stomach turned in knots. Not because I was afraid my captor would hear me, no, I was more afraid of what might answer back.

But I got nothing. Nothing in return. No movement, nothing.

So, I'd said it again, louder. *"Hello, can you hear me?"*

Nothing.

"Please," I begged. *"Maybe we can help each other."*

Nothing.

Not even a grunt, a sniff, a snort. This led me to believe that whatever was in the corner across from me was either already dead, or incapacitated... and probably pretty close to death. Honestly, I didn't know which scenario freaked me out more.

And then the terrifying thought... would I be next?

As the hours of pitch-black silence dragged on, my mind

began to wander. To play tricks on me. To see things, hear things, feel things next to me. A paralyzing fear of my own imagination. I'd close my eyes, only to see the exact same thing as when they were opened. So, I told myself I could never close them. What was worse? The nightmares that were surely to come if I were to fall asleep, or not being prepared for the nightmare that was lurking around me.

Hours, hours, and hours, I stared, blinking over and over, hoping that the visions when I opened my eyes would be different.

They weren't.

I'd spent the following day fighting with the cuffs and rusted metal chains, tracing where they'd been drilled deep into the rock. Blindly running my hands along the cold wall looking for something—*anything*—to use as a key or a weapon. I'd given up on calling out to whatever else was in that hole, and tried to force the grotesque images of what it might be out of my imagination. I'd imagined that it was a child, which incited a mixture of rage and sheer terror in me, or was it a grown woman, or man? Or, an animal of sorts? Maybe a dog. Murdered and skinned alive.

Whatever it was, it had lost a lot of blood.

Or maybe it was a secret science experiment of a half-man, half-beast monster. I swore I'd never watch another scary movie again. So, I focused on myself and my escape.

Eventually, I found two small, thin stones hugging the wall. I yelled out, *"Yes!"*, and began laughing hysterically. A crazy woman who'd just found the last marshmallow in the box of Lucky Charms. Giddy, like a toddler on Christmas morning... no, like a prisoner about to escape its solitary confinement.

Hope. That's what those two stones had given me. The priceless gift of hope.

With renewed energy, I began frantically sharpening them against each other. My plan was to make a shiv to either finagle my way out of the cuffs or kill the bastard if he got too close to me. I went at it with every bit of gusto as a mob boss in an Italian restaurant, rubbing the rocks together until my fingernails were ripped to shreds and the tips were raw with blisters.

After making the second—Day 2—nick on my wrist, I was a mess. My long, braided blonde hair was matted with sweat, dirt, and tears that had dried up long ago. I was weak, my mind drifting between a haze and a hyper-alertness that made my skin crawl. I could no longer feel the tips of my fingers, even though the stones were still as dull as a spoon. But it was *something.* Something to do with my time. A light. *Hope.*

I'd dug a small hole in the ground to use as a bathroom when I needed to, which wasn't often, thank God. I couldn't remember if I'd slept or not. If I had, it was only fleeting moments where my body had succumbed to the exhaustion of multiple adrenaline crashes. I'd seen my captor twice since I'd been thrown into that hellhole. Both times, I was given water and a protein bar. I never really saw him, only a dark silhouette of a man in front of a strategically placed flashlight. Even though he was nothing but an outline, I'd memorized every inch of him, from his six-feet tall frame to his fit, muscular body that told me he was someone who took pride in his appearance, his health.

Then, he'd leave again without so much as a single word. No rape, no torture, no taunting.

I was being held captive for a reason, and that had become clear to me. Given enough food and water to survive but nothing else.

Why, I had no idea.

I'd spent every second of every day trying to memorize everything around me, from the smell, the feel, the temperature, the sound of his boots against the dirt when he'd come back. Trying to put together clues to help me understand my situation.

I'd come to realize when it was day or night due to the noises outside the trap door. If I listened carefully, I could hear birds during the day time, and sometimes even squirrels. At night, it was cripplingly silent.

When I wasn't going at the rocks, I'd become fixated on the other presence in the room—the one I couldn't see, couldn't hear, never spoke back to me. Only that *smell.*

During a moment of weakness, I'd called out to it again, but with no luck. I told it that we'd make it through this, together.

Still, no response.

My skin had become hyper sensitive to even the slightest movement of air. It had to be, because that was my only warning that something was close by. Bugs, spiders, rats. Many little, disgusting, slithering creatures lived underground.

I was listening to the air above me, determining that night had fallen, when—

Thud, thud, thud.

Boots on the ground above.

Shit.

My heart slammed against my ribcage, a wave of blinding heat rolling through my body, followed by tingles and a watery sheen of sweat.

Not now, I begged myself, *not—*

Before I could finish my pep talk, a knot grabbed my throat, my pulse racing at breakneck speed. I pushed up against the rock wall and curled into a ball, gasping for breath that didn't seem to reach my lungs.

I'd had three panic attacks since I'd been in the hole, three debilitating, energy-zapping attacks that had left me breathless and frozen on the ground for hours after. Three in two days.

Countless in the last thirteen years.

Willing myself to fade away into the blackness, I pressed harder against the wall, thankful for the chill of it. Grateful once, for the coolness it provided against my skin.

I focused on my breathing, the buzz in my ears becoming louder with each wave of panic. But nothing could drown out the *clink* of the lock being removed from the door.

Then, the *creak* of the door. The blinding pool of light from his flashlight. The repetitive thud of his boots down the ladder, a drum, warning me of evil. Then, steps across the dirt. My body shook feverishly from head to toe as I watched his silhouette move across the room. But instead of tossing me a water and piece of cardboard, he passed me. My eyes widened, following the single beam of light across the cellar.

I was going to see it.

I was finally going to see what else was in that hole.

My heart jackhammered in my chest. I gripped the sharpest rock I'd carved in my palm. My eyes peeled open, even though my brain was telling me to look away. I didn't know if I could *handle* it. I didn't know if I wanted to put a face to this creature that had kept me company for forty-eight hours.

"Sit up." He spoke, his voice low, gravelly and eerily calm.

In slow motion, I watched him raise the flashlight.

And I froze.

Under the blinding, fluorescent beam lay a young woman, in nothing but a dingy bra and underwear chained to the wall, the same as I was. Except her pale, lifeless skin had red ribbons streaking her arms and legs from where she'd been sliced open. Her face was bruised and bloody, her hair matted to her head.

Her eyes were closed. Swollen or intentional, I couldn't tell. She was chained to a metal pole that ran alongside the rock, and along it were thousands of marks where she'd be clinking her chains, before obviously slipping back under in a lifeless state.

My stomach rolled.

"Sit up," he demanded, a ring of disgust to his voice.

When she didn't move, he kicked her.

Like a dead animal, her body flopped against the kick, then wobbled back in place.

"Shit," he muttered as he kneeled down next to her. "Sit up, I said."

I stared in horror as one of her eyes drifted open, then the other.

When he was satisfied she was still alive, he stood, then pulled his cell phone and something else from his belt. He unfolded the black contraption.

No.

My mouth gaped as the light from the cell phone illuminated her frail body as he positioned it into place on the tripod he'd just set up.

A camera stand. The guy was about to videotape whatever he was going to do to her.

Tears stung my eyes, from fear, shock, horror, absolute disbelief.

He pulled a gun from his belt. As he clicked on the

video, the light caught his forearm, highlighting a black *V* inked down it.

I gasped, paralyzed with visions from my past exploding through my head.

"Seventy-two hours..." He said as he stepped back and raised the gun.

I sucked in air to speak, scream, do *something*, but I couldn't form a single thought, sentence, plan, nothing.

"... deadline passed."

"No!" I screamed.

The blast echoed off the walls.

The camera turned off.

And I knew I had exactly twenty-four hours left.

3

AXEL

a cool breeze swept past me, that raw, piney scent pulling at old memories of hunting with my dad, family cookouts, campfires.

Not now, not anymore.

What was once a time of gathering, celebration, a time to admire the vibrant colors of Mother Nature, had been replaced with pain, desecration. Demise. A memory of an ending, the earth reminding me with its dying foliage, the slow suction of life from trees that once bloomed with energy. Now, twisted, gangly branches, bare with only a handful of brown, crumpled leaves hanging on until their time came. Eventually, they'd give up, fluttering to the cold, wet ground where their last shred of dignity was trampled by the earth's creatures, without giving it a second thought.

The days became shorter, nights longer.

The darkness overcoming light.

Yes, what was once my favorite season was now a symbol of death.

I was very familiar with death. Hell, I'd made an entire career of it. I grew up playing "war" in the woods with my brothers, using branches as guns, rocks as grenades, mud as face paint. Gage's gun was always the biggest branch, a prelude to his choice in women, by the way. It didn't matter if he could hold onto the thing, big to him always meant powerful. Gunner's was always the smallest, an extension of his arm, himself, which was fitting considering he turned into one of the best snipers in the country. Phoenix always wielded his branch as a knife. Not much better than hand to hand combat, he'd say. And mine, well, mine was the carefully selected knotted branch complete with night vision, dot sights, tactical lights, short and long range capability, and all the bells and whistles. Always be prepared for every scenario, that was my motto. I'd slip into the shadows, then climb the tallest tree, wait—for hours sometimes—and then pick off my brothers one by one, watching them drop like flies. Always had to send a few extra rounds into Gage, that stubborn bastard. It wasn't the size of your gun, it was how you used it. Your plan of attack. Self-restraint overcoming the natural human instinct of haste when it came to being hunted. See, I'd always considered my mind as much of a weapon as my fists, knife, gun, my crossbow. Even more deadly.

Patience, forethought, and follow-through was why I was undefeated at war, with my brothers when I was younger, and on the battlefield as an adult.

Undefeated.

Every fucking time.

I'd lost count of the lives I'd taken while in the military. Lost count, or purposefully forgotten, I wasn't sure which. It was a messed up way to live, and sometimes I wondered if karma was finally coming back to bite me in the ass. Because death was something I had accepted, had hardened to it. But when it involves your family, your blood, a part of you being ripped away before their season was up, well, that was something I wasn't willing to accept. Something that had a way of challenging every rational thought in a mind so carefully managed and monitored.

Something that made me want to attack, savagely, bathe in blood, rip souls from chests, not stopping until the last body was shredded to nothing but bones.

Yeah, I'd always been the cool, calm, collected Steele brother, no one questioned that, but over the last few weeks that patience was slipping away, poisoned by the need for revenge.

The universe was challenging me.

And it was in for one hell of a fight.

That day I was hellbent on leaving the poison behind, getting back to my roots. Recalibrating.

Little did I know, recalibrating was the exact opposite of what the universe had in mind for me. It was the day that changed my life forever.

I'd escaped to the woods for a hunt with practically nothing. A phone that only my brothers had access to—and that was only to provide updates as needed. No luxuries.

Exactly the way I liked it.

Squatted behind a bush, I forced myself to focus. Focus on the moment, the leaves rustling around me, static white noise breaking the drum of nature. A waving canopy of trees greedily absorbing the afternoon sunlight. It was a part of nature that most people would never see, never hear. But all you had to do was quiet yourself. Your body, your mind. Be still. For hours. Days, even. Wait. Wait until you were forgotten. Wait until the rhythm of nature settles around you, or if you're me, wait until your target comes into view.

Then strike.

An ambush predator is something that catches their prey by stealth or strategy, rather than by speed or strength. Thanks to my career—previous career, I should say—I was skilled on all counts. Stealth, strategy, speed, and strength. Life or death was a concept I wasn't allowed in the Marines, because death was always one bullet away. Life was the only option. The past life where I saw things no horror movie could dream up, a life where I watched my comrades die next to me; children, women, slaughtered.

To survive was to be lethal. To survive was to be the best.

And I was the fucking best.

No one held a candle to my ability to wait out a target.

I sat and waited. Silently. Patiently. I wore head-to-toe camo, dirt-covered ATAC boots, and dried mud over every inch of my exposed skin. Face paint was for pussies. I blended into my surroundings with nothing but the whites of my eyes to give me away. I'd gained the trust of the nature around me. I *was my surroundings.*

One of the deadliest ambush predators is the Komodo dragon. These one-hundred and fifty pound bastards are known to stalk their prey for sometimes days at a time. A singular focus, lying in wait. Most humans don't have that kind of patience. No, we live in an instant gratification society where the fruits of our labor are expected after whatever deed we'd convinced ourselves was a good one. The need to sate our cravings, feed our impulses, whether food, drugs, sex, money—pick your poison—outweighs all else. We've convinced ourselves that it's *ours,* that we *deserve* it. We have to have it, right then. Fast. Now. An all-consuming greed that takes over. Never taking a second to consider, to think, plan, strategize. To make a conscious decision. A life driven by cravings and impulses is a dangerous way to live. Trust me. I'd built an entire life around emotional discipline. Thinking, strategizing, making calculated decisions. Tireless dedication to whatever I was hunting.

Like I was right then.

Like the Komodo Dragon.

After the Komodo decides it's time to strike, the dragon doesn't go for a quick kill like a lion, or a panther. He doesn't go for the neck. No, when this hunter strikes, he inflicts massive wounds by a 'grip and rip' method, shredding and eviscerating your skin like strings of cheese. A brutal, conscious attack. You might get away, and most do, but that fleeting moment of hope is only temporary. Because the Komodo has injected a deadly poison into your bloodstream guaranteeing you a slow, agonizing death filled with searing pain, nausea, and hallucinations that go on for hours.

But he's not done.

The Komodo is secretly, stealthily stalking you, tracking his injured prey for miles before finally, *finally,* indulging.

Commitment.

Patience.

Vengeance.

I had all three in fucking spades.

The only difference in the Komodo and me at that moment? The endgame. The Komodo hunted to survive. At that moment, I hunted to release. A target to funnel the rage that had been coursing through my veins over the last two weeks. That day, I hunted to forget.

A thorn from the bush I was crouched behind scraped across my face for the hundredth time. I was numb to the sting at that point. And that was nothing compared to the leg cramps that were coming every handful of minutes. A constant dull pain marked by a shot of lightning up my muscle. Not that I gave a shit. I loved it. I loved the pain. I *needed* it. It reminded me of the life I used to have, the one I used to love. God, I missed the Marines. I embraced the pain, gritting through it with a respect for its dedication. Respect for its ability to remind me that I was strong. Stronger than anxiety, depression, fear. That I could overcome the circumstances that had turned my world upside down.

And I would.

Another gust of cool air against my heated skin. Yellow, orange, and red leaves rained down on me, swaying back and forth in the wind, blocking my target. I blinked, refocused, and shifted my crossbow that I'd perched between two branches. A centipede slithered across my mud-caked boot. Careful not to move my head, I glanced down, only moving the dots of my pupils. I didn't much care for centipedes. Anything with a hundred and seventy-seven pairs of anything made my skin crawl. Pun unintended.

I felt the tingle of another cramp, grit my teeth and willed it away.

The temperatures had dropped with the late afternoon, I guessed somewhere in the mid-sixties, with promises of sinking into the fifties later that week. Autumn was bipolar bitch in the Ozarks.

Beams from the slanting sun shot out from the neighboring mountain beyond a steep ravine about a hundred yards out. Shimmering dapples of light swayed along the forest floor, a constant movement, a constant distraction. Maybe for the seasoned hunter.

Not me.

My grip tightened around my crossbow as I narrowed my sights. My fingers tingled, my pulse threatening to pick up with the inevitable adrenaline rush that comes with hitting your target.

A duo of squirrels chased each other up a nearby pine tree, chittering, chattering.

A crow, as black as night, called out.

My target—a 36-point whitetail—continued to graze, unaware of the prey stalking him through the forest. He moved forward, a tree trunk blocking my shot.

My eye narrowed, not only with annoyance, but admiration as well. It was his M.O. As quickly as he'd entered my crosshairs, giving me a second to focus, he'd move again. Every *single time*. Little did he know the challenge was only strengthening my resolve.

I shifted to the balls of my feet, mainly to get feeling back into my toes. I closed my eyes, took a quick breath, then focused again on the target.

Commitment, patience.

No mercy.

4

AXEL

I needed a release. We all did. And this was going to be mine.

Cassi had caught my attention four months earlier when Wolf, former Marine turned head of security for Steele Shadows, had spotted him on one of our security cams. Cassi was an impressive beast, but his rack had more than doubled since then—and we all know how much the Steele brothers enjoyed a decent rack. His name was short for Cassiopeia, a nod to the white markings on his chest that were identical to the constellation. My brothers couldn't see it, but I could, clear as day. And as ol' Cassi grew into his rack, the markings became more prominent, like a work of art right there on his chest.

Hypnotized by the beast, I'd started watching Cassi since the day Wolf discovered him. Taking note of his daily routes, his routines, habits. His impressive harem that would make Gage jealous. Cassi was nothing short of alpha —confident, strong, a silent force to be reckoned with. Something about that animal reminded me of myself. Crazy, I know.

Cassi had grown into the biggest buck I'd ever seen, and possibly a Steele record.

Over the months, I'd let him be, warning my brothers that he was mine, whatever that meant. But it wasn't until that day that I began stalking him, ready to take the shot. Perhaps it was timing, perhaps it was fate.

Perhaps I was losing my fucking mind.

Under the circumstances that wasn't hard to imagine.

I'd been out in the woods for two days at that point—or was it three? I didn't know, didn't care—with nothing but my crossbow, gun, bullets, water, a few MRE's, and a roll of toilet paper. No sleeping bag, blanket. No bullshit. I'd taken a quick dip in the creek the day before, but other than that I was at nature's mercy. To do with what she pleased. My five o'clock shadow had filled in, almost to a full beard, the hair I hadn't cut since I left the Marines was mussed, dirty, and curling around my ears. My arms, legs, covered in dirt, mud, shit.

But, the last two nights... I'd actually slept—for the first time in two weeks. Right there under the stars, I'd slept like a baby. The twelve nights before had been spent pacing the house, the grounds, the compound, tossing and turning in my air-conditioned room and king-sized bed. Trying to control the rage, the spinning mind that was telling me pack up my arsenal of guns and blaze through town demanding answers to questions that were nothing more than a billion pieces of a loose puzzle.

Ever since I was a little boy, I remember having spinning thoughts. An overactive mind that analyzed and dissected every single thing around me. I was always on *go*. Always working toward whatever goal I'd set for myself that day, week, month, year, never resting until it was accomplished. Then, I was on to the next. Challenging myself. Others around me. I could always do better; be better. And so I was. I poured my soul into everything I did, even if it was going to kill me. And believe me, a few times it came close.

I was an analytical person to the core. I could solve a problem. Anything you could throw me, I'd find the fastest, most efficient way through it. Facts, black and white facts were my jam. Women—a constant shade of gray—were a completely different story. I knew how to treat one, handle one—trust me there—and satisfy one until they'd beg for more, but emotions? Relationships? The ups and downs that came with the female psyche? No thank you. Women were not black and white creatures, women were a kaleido-scope of swirling rainbows constantly changing, mixing. I couldn't keep up. Actually yeah, I could. Of course I could, I just didn't want to.

Gunner told me I lacked a sensitivity chip. Empathy, whatever. The truth was, he wasn't that far off. Comforting, consoling, reassuring wasn't my thing. I was a 'put on your big girl panties' kind of guy, which, trust me, didn't go over well with women. When I'd finally realized my "impersonal personality" didn't mix well with anything other than a few nights in the bedroom, I'd slipped seamlessly into the Steele family legacy of ladies' men, and never looked back. Enjoy the beauty, the spirit of a woman, then the next. Simple as that.

Simple.

Besides, most of my time was filled watching out for my brothers, and trust me, that was a full-time job. But *that* I could do. We were a pack, my brothers and I, each of us taking a bullet for the other. We were ride or die, and wouldn't have it any other way.

Except I was always a little bit different.

When you're born into a family of jacked-up alpha

males, natural sibling competition is amped up a few thousand notches. While my brothers were competing to be the first place winner of whatever we were doing, I was always competing with myself. How could I beat my previous best? What other angle could I take to get this accomplished? And over the years, I'd found that I was one hell of an adversary. So, the challenge, pushing my limits, was constant.

I'd started fasting when I was ten. Removing one craving a month, just to prove myself that I could. It started with food, but quickly expanded to things I desired the most. Television, internet, booze, sex. Fasting was a way to keep me on my toes, remind me that I was more than my cravings, my impulses. That I was stronger than them. My longest food fast was thirteen days where I backpacked through the Andes Mountains, with nothing but a gun, water purification tablets and a handful of trail mix. A spiritual journey, whatever, but it was a pivotal point in my life, testing my limits, embracing who I was. How I was different than most other guys.

While my brothers were wrestling, shooting, backroading, fixing cars, I was always reading. I'd read anything I could get my hands on. Biographies, political thrillers, good ol' whodunit mysteries were always good for an escape. Hell, I'd even read a few women's fictions... a decision that cost Gunner a black eye when he'd mocked me for it.

He didn't make that mistake again. *Are you there God, it's me Margaret* sat on his nightstand for a week just to punctuate his narrow mindedness.

This restless drive for excellence served me well in my life, though. I worked my ass off in school, graduating valedictorian. Unlike my brothers, I went to college and studied computer science and physics, graduating magna cum laude before following in our father's footsteps and joining the

Marines. Along with the rest of my brothers, we were a part of an elite black ops team within MARSOC. I was promoted to team leader, specializing in reconnaissance, surpassing my twin brother, Gage, earning both his respect and irritation. For fifteen years, my brothers and I fought together, dedicating our lives to this beautiful country.

Until our dad died and we'd come home to take over his private security firm.

That was a year ago.

And if the last year wasn't bad enough, the last fourteen days were like the nuclear bomb, finishing off what we thought was our worst nightmare come true.

I'd spent every second buried in my computer, researching, tracking the bastard who decided to attack our family.

Hunting.

But when frustration, lack of sleep, lack of food, and the exhaustion caught up—and I threw my computer against the wall—Gage decided I needed a break.

So there I was. In the middle of the Ozark Mountains.

A snake slithered next to me, either not noticing or not caring that I was there. I assumed the latter. He knew he wasn't my target, and he was probably getting as restless as I was.

My jaw clenched as I aimed the tip of my arrow at the center of Cassi's heart.

The woods fell still around me, as if time froze.

Not a single sound, breeze, nothing.

It was time.

With my crossbow steady on my shoulder, I dipped my chin and narrowed my eyes. My finger slid over the trigger.

True to form, Cassi swayed a bit, a constant challenge, but I followed that heart.

A slight inhale.

My finger started to squeeze the trigger.

Cassi froze. Every muscle in his thick, sculpted body tensed as he raised his head.

My heart skipped a beat. I had the perfect shot.

Now. Now, Axel, now is the time.

The beast turned his head.

I blinked.

My gaze lifted from his heart and met his beady black eyes.

My pulse drummed as we stared at each other.

My finger slacked.

The bow dipped.

I swear to God Cassi grinned before turning and gracefully leaping away until those 36 points disappeared into the mountains.

I dropped my bow, staring into the woods.

What. The Fuck. Was That?

I blinked again, my methodic mind trying to understand why the hell I didn't pull the trigger.

I'd *had* him. The elusive bastard I'd been watching for *months.*

Right in my freaking crosshairs.

I found myself wanting to track him again, chase him down, but for what? I'd had the shot. That was it.

And I'd chosen not to take it.

Yep, I was losing my fucking mind. That was the only answer.

My chin lifted along with my sixth sense. Brow cocked, I turned into a stone whizzing through the air, bouncing directly off my forehead.

"Pussy." Grinning, Gage emerged from the underbrush where, despite his bright red T-shirt and tactical pants, the guy had been invisible and undetectable to every creature around him. Except for me, of course. His eyes were heavy and shaded, puffy with emotional turmoil and sleepless nights. I knew mine were, too.

He stepped over. "Was that Cassi?"

"Yep."

"Why didn't you take the shot?"

Irritated, I secured my crossbow onto my pack and slipped it around my shoulders. "Wasn't clear," I lied.

"Bullshit." He wrinkled his nose and took a step back. "And God, you stink."

I chugged a bottle of water and hurled it at his head. "Thanks. And, you're slipping, Gage. Ol' man Erikson probably heard you sneaking through the woods. Hell, Sake could've heard you."

"What does Sake have to do with this?"

Sake was the name given to a squid—yeah, literally, a squid—Gage had been talked into buying after having one too many *sakes* at a Japanese restaurant while on leave. He loved that damn thing and kept her in an aquarium in the library because he felt like she liked to be around books.

"Because Sake can't hear. I'm saying you were so damn loud..."

"What do you mean she can't hear?"

"Squid are deaf, you idiot."

"What? Are you serious?"

"Deaf serious."

"You never liked her and she knows it. You could've said a rattlesnake or something."

"Rattlesnakes aren't deaf."

"They don't have ears."

"They do have ears, not ear flaps. They have tiny holes in the side of their head with fully formed inner ears... Jesus did you sleep through school?"

A devilish grin crossed my brother's face. "You bet I did."

"Well try to have sex with a science teacher next time."

"Ahhhh," Gage gazed lustfully up at the sky. "Mrs. Schmidt."

I grinned. Take away the wide-rimmed glasses and seventeen pounds of chalk that always covered her clothes, and the German import could have been in a Motley Crew video. I still wasn't sure if the rumors that Gage had slept with her were true. Regardless, it appeared those days were long behind my twin brother now.

"Speaking of sleeping with smart women, have you made it out of the bedroom lately?"

The sheepish smile that crossed Gage's face took me by surprise. My brother had it bad. Madly in love with a prosecuting attorney named Niki whose life he'd saved two weeks earlier.

"Niki's heading back to work today, so..."

"So, you'll see less of her now?"

A grunt and obvious refrain of eye contact.

My eyebrows tipped up. *"Gage..."*

He cleared his throat.

"Gage... don't fucking tell me you asked her to marry you."

"What?" His neck snapped in my direction like a bomb had gone off. "No. *No. Jesus,* man. *No.*" He laughed. "God, Dallas would have my hide."

Damn right she would. Our over-protective stepmother always had her hands in our business, always looking out for us, watching over us. And since she'd become a widow? Her need to be in our lives was only outweighed by her need for new handbags.

"What is it, then?" I asked my brother. "What aren't you telling me?"

He looked up at the trees for a moment before saying, "I'm thinking about moving in with her."

My jaw dropped. Ever since leaving the military and moving back to Berry Springs, we lived on the compound, together. It wasn't even a question. The house was so massive we all had our own wings. We were together. Finding our ways through the muck *together.*

"Don't look at me like that."

I shook out of my shocked stupor, reminding myself that we all needed to grow up and leave the nest at some point. "Sorry." I gripped his shoulder. "No, it's good for you. She's good for you."

"Thanks. And yeah, she is. She's... she's really been there for me since... you know."

Yeah, I knew. And I also knew of the little twinges of jealously I'd gotten knowing my brother had someone to help him through the last few weeks.

He continued, "You know, Ax, we're not gone three hundred days a year anymore. We have a home base now, a different life."

I shifted my weight, unsure where he was going with that, but having a good feeling I didn't want to go with him.

He continued, "You know... it's not bad having someone."

I stared at him.

"I'm just saying, you should try it, is all. Find a good woman."

I snorted and stepped past him. "What the fuck man? Come on. And pick up your balls from the dirt before you leave."

A chuckle behind me, then he caught up with me.

"You come out here to tell me you're a changed man, Gage?"

"No, I came out here to drag your ass home."

My jaw twitched. Home. The one place I didn't want to be. "No thanks, bro. Got another night in me out here."

"Dude the trees are suffering enough."

I grinned.

"Because air pollution... you stink so bad—"

"I got it. I got it."

"Also, we've got an update meeting tomorrow morning."

I halted. "An update meeting isn't why you're dragging me home, Gage."

He turned toward me, his eyes narrowed in a look I'd seen before.

A look that had my gut clenching.

"Ax. There's been developments."

5

AXEL

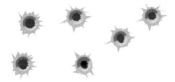

"*T*alk."

"We got the official ballistics report back from the state crime lab." We started through the woods. "Didn't tell us much that we didn't know—confirmed the bullet was a .380, likely shot from a Ruger, based on the pin markings on the casing. One shot, one bullet, shot at a one-seventy degree angle, directly into Phoenix's brain."

"Okay, so that matches the gun that was in his hand when you found him. Did the markings from the casing line up with that gun?"

"According to the report, yes."

I shook my head.

Gage continued, *"And,* the fingerprints on the magazine also match the gun he was holding."

I clenched my teeth. "They're sure?"

"Yes. Gun was his, prints were his. It's confirmed now."

Dammit. "Is Lieutenant Colson going to have Cross take a look at the gun?"

Gage nodded. "Under the table, yeah. Guy's bogged

down, though, but said he'd make it top priority when he got it."

A former Marine himself, Wesley Cross was the town's ballistics expert turned gun manufacturing business owner, and was the local PD's go-to guy for 'off the books' insight. No one was better than Cross when it came to analyzing guns. Not even the state crime lab geeks.

I ran my fingers through my hair. A few leaves fell out. "One- seventy angle you say?"

A moment passed by without eye contact. "Yep."

I blew out a breath. This new, "confirmed" information didn't bode well for our theory that our oldest brother *hadn't* wanted to kill himself. I'd been hoping for a deeper angle, one that would indicate that my brother had been shot while someone stood over him. That it was all a setup. But this angle would be inconclusive to that theory. It was plausible that Feen could have shot himself at that angle, *or,* that someone else did it.

I closed my eyes and pictured the scene from two weeks earlier. It was burned into my brain. From only the glow of the computers, to my brother, slumped over our dad's chair with a single trail of blood running down his neck, to Gage going apeshit next to him.

The scene screamed suicide. It suggested that my brother couldn't take the emotional toll from our father's death a year earlier, and had decided to end his life by sticking a gun to his forehead and pulling the trigger. But Gage, Gunner, and I knew the real story. The real story was that Phoenix had been knee-deep in researching the theory that our dad didn't die of a heart attack as the autopsy report had said—that Duke Steele, former director of the National Security Agency, was murdered after being caught secretly tracking an international assassin.

No, my brother's scene, and the evidence, all pointed to him wanting to end his own life. The case that was being built suggested that Phoenix had become a different person after dad was killed—this much was true. He'd become all-consumed with his theory that dad had been murdered. Then, a few days after the one year anniversary of dad's death, Phoenix grabbed his Ruger, took it up to dad's office and pulled the trigger. The immediate evidence supported this theory.

The tox report confirmed that there were no traces of drugs in Feen's system, debunking one of our theories that maybe he'd been drugged.

All signs pointed to Phoenix Steele shooting himself.

Just like all signs pointed to Dad dying of a heart attack.

Except none if it were true.

The local PD had already closed the case on dad, and I had no doubt that they would do the same to Feen's by the end of the week. So, my brothers and I decided to let the local PD do their job, determine what they will, while we secretly tracked the son of a bitch who was attacking our family. With all odds against us.

A scenario we were very familiar with.

"How is he?" I asked.

"The same. The drain tubes are controlling the swelling. It could go either way."

"Did the doctor say how long they intend to keep him under?"

"No. I get the vibe things are too up in the air right now."

I nodded, my gut clenching.

Yes, Phoenix Steele was still alive. Clinging to life by a thread.

The bullet had gone through the upper right quadrant of Feen's forehead, fracturing the skull and embedding into the brain. An MRI determined that the bullet lodged instantly, without bouncing around in the brain, which would have certainly caused sudden death. That was the first one in a million. The second was that no skull shards or fragments pierced the brain, which would have caused more damage. The third one in a million was that Feen was the strongest mother fucker on the planet and not even a bullet to the brain could bring him down.

In terms of a gunshot wound to the head, Feen had been one lucky bastard, although it didn't appear that way from the outside looking in. Our oldest brother remained in ICU, in critical condition, in a medically induced coma with drains, wires, and IV's flowing in and out of every inch of his body.

My brother had flat-lined three times since Gage had found him two weeks ago.

And fucking came back from each one.

To say he was lucky is the understatement of the century. To say what his quality of life would be after this was the big question. We'd been prepped for everything from the "vegetable state," to Feen waking up with the mental capacity of a one-year old, spending the rest of his life relearning the simple basics of life, if his brain would even allow for it. It would be another "one in a million" for Feen to wake up and regain a normal life.

I liked those odds.

The right side of the brain controls attention, memory, reasoning, and problem solving. So, that's what we were up against. But it was okay, Feen wasn't great at half those skills anyway. Bottomline was that along with the dead brain tissue that was removed, an MRI confirmed damage to the brain, so we knew repercussions were definite. We just didn't know how bad.

And that was assuming he'd pull through.

Ever since that day, the entire family took shifts, sitting with him in the hospital. Four hour rotating shifts... until one of us deemed another needed a few days break. I guess throwing a computer against the wall indicated that my turn for forty-eight was due.

My next shift was tomorrow morning.

"What about Wolf?" I asked. "Has he made headway on the Knight Fox?"

"Not since you destroyed your computer in a dumbass fit of rage."

"Hey, I said I was sorry about that."

"So was he. Do you know how much security he'd loaded onto that thing? Anyway, he ordered you a new one. Came in yesterday. Should be ready for you today, to pick up where you left off."

Where I'd left off was hitting a wall around every corner in tracking the elusive Knight Fox, the name associated with the man we believed killed dad, and tried to kill Phoenix. Over the last two weeks, one thing had become evident—we were not dealing with an amateur. The Knight Fox covered his tracks expertly. So expertly in fact, it was his only mistake thus far. Only a few people knew their way around computer code like The Fox did. Our dad, myself, and our head of security, Wolf, were three of those people. We also had the bead on a small network of coding geniuses and had been picking away at that list. It was never-ending. And it would never end. Not until we found the man responsible for attacking our family.

Gage and I walked in silence, splashing through a creek at the base of the mountain. The late afternoon sun had dipped below the mountain, with twilight hot on its heels. The breeze had picked up along with a chill in the air.

I kept an eye out for Cassi, to redeem myself, perhaps. But if I knew anything about that beast, it would be a long while until he showed his rack around the house again.

"Dude, do you know where we are?" Despite Gage's peak physical condition, the guy appeared winded trekking up the steep mountain. He'd been burning his energy in the bedroom if I had to guess. Lucky bastard.

I still couldn't believe my twin brother was thinking about settling down. Moving in with a woman? The thought was exciting and unnerving at the same time. Exciting for him. Unnerving for me. Not only because a part of me felt like I might lose my brother, but it would be a constant flashing light in my face telling me it was time I settled down.

And that thought made me want to reach into Gage's back pocket and chug the rest of the whiskey in the flask he didn't know I'd noticed.

I maneuvered around a rocky dip in the terrain, grabbing onto a sapling to toss myself over. Gage mimicked— and almost face planted. I grinned.

"We're off Red Rock Trail." I nodded to the break in trees in the distance. We'd veered off the trail and I wondered if it was because Gage didn't want anyone seeing me in the condition I was.

"Going to get dark soon. How much longer to your truck?"

"'Bout two miles. Need me to carry you?"

This earned me another rock to the head.

I stopped cold, as did Gage.

My instinct piqued, every inch of my body instantly on alert.

My brother and I looked at each other as we listened,

our focus moving beyond the wind rustling through the leaves.

"You hear that?"

"Yeah." I pulled my SIG from the holster on my belt.

"It's a woman. Screaming."

"Yeah. I hear it."

We pivoted and followed the sound, stepping through the thick brush as a snake through the water, our heads on a swivel. Guns in hand, we moved toward the noise, my increased pulse telling me something wasn't right.

The screaming stopped.

We stopped, squatted, froze.

A solid two minutes slid by as nature resumed around us.

My fingers began to tingle around the hilt of my gun. Someone was in trouble—a woman—and I was one-hundred percent sure of it.

Another yell, this one crying out. I stood, moved toward the sound, quicker this time. I didn't hear Gage behind me, but knew he was there.

We came up on a clearing and paused to listen.

Another muffled scream. My head snapped toward the sound, focusing on a large boulder at the edge of the clearing.

"Ready?" Gage scanned the woods circling us.

I nodded and had to keep myself from jogging to the rock. A cool gust of wind swept up my back, like a hand pushing me forward. Guiding me.

Guns raised, we breached the tree line and approached the boulder, then did a one-eighty. Gage stayed in position while I climbed up and slid over, and found a rusted trap door.

"There's an underground cellar here." I kneeled down and put my hand on the trap door.

"A *what?*"

"A door. Locked."

"Out here?"

"I'm staring at it."

A spine-chilling scream called out from beyond the door. My brother's eyes met mine, wide, hyper-alert. He took another look around, then met me by the door.

I assessed the lock, the woman inside now screaming inaudible pleas from beyond the metal. My pulse was racing at that point. I turned over the lock in my hands.

"Here, let me..." Gage grabbed a lock pick from the keys dangling from my bag and began picking it.

The woman was hysterical, and despite my ability to remain cool under pressure, the hair on the back of my neck stood up with each scream. I glanced up at the darkening sky.

"Fuck this. Get back." I said.

"You're not serious."

"Get back."

Gage moved to the side as I raised my gun and blasted the lock.

The screams stopped.

My hand was unsteady as I removed the broken pieces from the door.

"Keep a lookout." I said over my shoulder.

Gage nodded.

I'll never forget the smell as I opened that door. It was a scent I'd come across dozens of times while executing hostage raids overseas. A wave of adrenaline pulsed through me. You never knew what you'd find beyond that smell. More often than not, it was one of the few things that used to keep me up at night. Little did I know this one was going to be the exact same, for many different reasons.

The black hole in the earth went silent, still, as if it had been a ghost crying out earlier.

My brother shifted his gaze from his watch over the woods. "How deep?"

"I'd say fifteen feet."

I called out but was met with silence. Not so much of a shuffle sounded from the darkness.

I grabbed the sides of the hole. "I'm going down."

6

AXEL

*G*age nodded. "I'll cover your six."

I pulled a flashlight from my pack, clicked it on, and stuck it in my mouth. SIG in one hand, I braced myself on the door frame, then stepped down the ladder.

It was as black as tar so I funneled my attention to my hearing, as we'd been trained to do. Again, no movement, not even labored breath of whoever had been screaming her lungs out.

I landed on the dirt floor and raised the light along with the barrel of my gun. I scanned the gray, wet, rock walls, a spotlight cutting through the blackness.

Like slow motion, a pale, limp foot came into view, covered in dirt and dried blood. My finger slid over the trigger, flashbacks of my past life kicking my heartbeat into full blast. Her legs, sliced to shreds, the veins dark against grey skin. The woman laid on her side in nothing but a bra and panties, her arms crossed over her chest in one final desperate attempt to shield her body from the torture it had endured for multiple days, I guessed. And her face, her expression frozen in an emotionless plea under a mess of matted blonde hair.

A single streak of blood led to the bullet hole in her forehead.

This wasn't the woman who'd been screaming moments earlier.

My ears focused to my backside as I continued to sweep the light over the walls, turning a one-eighty on my heels.

... until a smudged jogging shoe reflected in the beam.

My heart skipped a beat as the woman came into view.

Pressed against the wall, the light reflected in ice-blue eyes the size of golf balls, against pale, dirt-covered skin and platinum blonde hair tangled with dirt and leaves. She stared at me, motionless, a mixture of shock, fear, trepidation. My gaze shifted to the dried blood coloring the metal cuffs secured around her wrists and ankles. In one hand, she clutched a thin, dull rock as a child would their favorite teddy bear.

"Hi, there. You're going to be okay." Keeping my light and eyes on her, I slid my gun back into the holster. "I'm going to get you out of here."

I edged closer, angling the light so that it wasn't blinding her, but knowing all she saw of me was a large, black silhouette.

The woman was terrified. Rightly so.

"What's your name?" I asked inching closer.

Her lips parted, but no words came out. She sat frozen, her eyes darting to each of my movements. It was a look I'd seen many, many times before.

"Bro, you alright?"

Her gaze flickered toward my brother's voice outside the door, then focused back on me.

"Bro?"

"What's your name?" I repeated softly as I squatted in front of her.

She blinked, then like a shot of epinephrine, her chest kicked started, into deep, raspy breaths.

"Erika," she pushed in a desperate, gritty tone. "My name is Erika... My name is Erika," she repeated, louder as if reminding herself that she wasn't in a dream.

"Erika, okay, that's a beautiful name. I'm here to get you out of here. Is that okay?"

She nodded frantically but her body didn't move, not a single flinch—and that concerned me.

"Bro."

"I'm good," I hollered back calmly so not to startle her. "We're gonna need a medic."

"... How—"

"One for two."

"... On it."

"I'm going to take a look at the chains, is that okay?"

"Yes." Her voice cracked. "He has keys. There's a key for them."

"Don't worry, we won't need them."

I lifted her hand. She was freezing to the touch. Anger began to simmer. The broken skin was infected with God knew what. I shifted and started to crab-walk to her foot.

"Wait." She gasped, horror flashing on her face.

I froze mid-step.

"Stop."

I lifted my hands, palms hands out. "Okay. Why?"

"I..." tears welled with the panic in her eyes. "There's..."

I followed her gaze to the small hole she'd dug in the dirt. A knot formed in my throat. I pushed it away with a smile. "Don't worry about that, sweetheart." Then, I thoughtfully cocked my head. "Actually I kind of need to go. Do you mind…"

The corner of her lip curled next to the tear that ran down it. My fucking heart kicked.

I winked. She smiled sheepishly before looking down.

"Okay, let's get you out of here and into a real bathroom."

She nodded, and began pulling at her cuffs. I laid my hand over hers and waited for her to look up at me. When she did, my stomach dropped.

"I'll handle it." I had to force the damn words out. "Okay?"

She stared back with the first sign of life, a spark in those aqua eyes. They were hypnotic, like swirling patterns of fire and ice, pinning me and turning me into a tongue-tied Neanderthal.

It was the first moment I realized how beautiful she was. Behind all that dirt and panic.

And looking back, the first moment of many that left my head spinning like a top.

I replaced my focus on her wrists, noticing the colorful artwork of tattoos on her arms, a juxtaposition to the angel-like pixie face and smattering of freckles over her nose. Initially, I guessed she was mid-twenties, but the story behind her eyes said anything but a struggling new adult. I settled with early thirties.

I grabbed my lock pick and went to work on each cuff, avoiding the oozing wounds while reigning in the rage that boiled up with each one. She didn't flinch, didn't whine, didn't whimper, simply stared at me with an expression that had my hand slipping a few times.

A ticking time bomb strapped to a pair of four-year-old twins didn't break my concentration once. A five-foot-two, hundred pound silent statue made my job almost impossible.

It threw me, that I'll admit.

"You good?" Gage yelled down from above, the slightest pitch in his voice telling me he was anxious to know what was taking so long.

With a *clink*, the first cuff opened.

Erika winced and pulled her arm to her chest, closed her eyes and exhaled. I wanted to wrap her in my arms.

Christ.

I grit my teeth and focused on the job at hand. "Medic ETA?" I hollered up.

"Guessing 10 minutes but they've got to transfer to ATV's to get here. Park rangers are on their way."

The other cuff gave and I moved onto her feet. She'd fallen completely silent, motionless. I watched her for a minute, her face tilted to the ceiling, the heavy inhale, heavy exhale. Her oozing palm lay open on her thigh, her expression soft with each deep breath. It took me a minute but I realized she was doing some sort of meditation. And I continued to watch her in astonishment of the self-control in the middle of a nightmare. A tingle brewed in the depths of me, something deep inside as I watched each breath. The slow parting of her lips.

I cleared my throat and went back to work on the cuffs.

"I saw it," she finally whispered, breaking the silence. The tone of her voice told me exactly what she was referring to. I didn't need to ask. I looked up at her, continuing to work on her left foot.

"It will fade," I said.

"I don't think so."

It would, I wanted to tell her again. The vivid colors of watching another human being take their last breath would fade, but the picture would remain, only to reveal itself in your deepest sleep, on loop, for the rest of your life. Imprinting onto your soul, a brief moment in time, a blip, that would change the course of your future. Change who you were to the very core.

I didn't lie. Yes, it would fade, but it would always be there.

Death had a way of lingering.

The after-effects everlasting.

And I needed to pull her focus away from the nightmare she was reliving.

"Tell me about your tattoos. The one above your wrist."

A second passed as she stared at her skin, the question taking a moment to register. "It's a star constellation."

"It's Cassiopeia."

"That's right."

I nodded and looked down in an effort not to stare. At her, at the woman with the Cassiopeia tattoo. I'd noticed almost immediately. The odds...

"I've always been fascinated with astrology, Greek mythology," she said, her voice a bit stronger, grateful to be pulled away from the moment. "The story of Cassiopeia always stuck with me. A beautiful, envied queen thought to have it all, but inside she was nothing more than an insecure fraud who placed vanity above all else." She paused. "The arrogance, exuberant lifestyle, lead her to an eternity of blackness."

"But in an ironic twist, the constellation is one of the most recognized star patterns in the world, marveled at by almost everyone, and used by many as a map to gauge their location. It's also part of the Milky Way, the Messier, star clusters, and remnants of a supernova. So, even in her exile, she's still exquisite." My gaze met hers. "True beauty shines through even the darkest of times."

She blinked slowly, the softest smile reaching her eyes.

The grumble of four-wheelers pulled our attention to the trap door.

"That'll be the Calvary." The cuff popped and I moved to the right. "You're almost out of here."

"Medic's here. I'm coming down." Gage yelled down as his body shadowed the door.

"What's your name?" She asked me.

"Axel."

"Axel," she repeated in a whisper before closing her eyes and leaning her head against the wall.

7

AXEL

Four days later...

P op, pop, pop!
        The sound of gunfire in the distance told me Gunner was at it again. The guy spent every spare second of his life at the range since our father's death. The only time he left the compound was to take his shift at the hospital or to get more ammo. Sometimes hit the bar. I got it, though, something about blasting a hole through the center of a target had a calming effect like nothing else.

It had been a day filled with meetings and client calls. Business was booming. A lot of sickos out there, and in some cases, a lot of paranoid panophobiacs. Everyone needed protection.

The last few weeks had felt endless, but we'd picked up the pieces, as we always did, and put one foot in front of the other. Took care of business, which was exactly what I was doing at that moment.

The slanting sun shadowed the woods around me, taking the mild temperatures with it. I was on my nightly perimeter check of the property. Some days I did the check on a four-wheeler, some days, one of the horses, that day, I'd parked at the tree line and decided to go on foot.

I needed to feel my feet on solid ground, needed to get the blood pumping, fresh air in my lungs, and push out the monotonous work day that involved phone calls and computers instead of guns and radios. Although it had been a year, I hadn't adjusted to my new life in business, and that was one hell of an understatement.

A gust of wind whipped past me, the crisp air scented with cedar. A thousand leaves rained down around me—and that's when I saw him. Hidden behind a thicket of trees, Cassi and his thirty-six points staring straight at me.

Cassiopeia.

A pair of ice-blue eyes flashed through my head as they'd done a million times over the last four days. And this unreasonable obsession was compounded two days ago when I received a card in the mail.

Mr. Steele,

I want to thank you for saving my life. Although words cannot express my ultimate gratitude, I hope this helps.

It brought me hope during the darkest of times, and maybe someday will do the same for you.

"True beauty shines through even the darkest of times"
  -Erika Zajac

.   .   .

When I'd tipped up the envelope a small, thin stone tumbled into my palm, whittled to a point at the tip. It was the stone Erika had carved while planning her escape. The stone she didn't need to use because I came along. And as if my shock needed any more amplification, drilled onto one side was five dots, in the shape of the star constellation of Cassiopeia.

I'd held that thing in my palm for a solid five minutes, my mouth gaping open

Cassiopeia... the darkest of times.

Hope.

The universe was messing with me. Hard core.

As if she'd put some kind of voodoo on me, no matter what I did, what I drank, I couldn't get Erika Zajac off my mind, which was precisely why I needed to. Which was precisely my goal that evening.

A black crow spun out of the tree above me, its wings flapping wildly against the darkening sky. Cassi turned and ran, disappearing into the shadows.

Bastard.

I clenched my jaw and pressed on, walking the property line, each step faster, harder, against the pine needles crunching below me. Each step like a turning handle winding me tighter and tighter until I was about to pop. I was a fucking mess. A ball of energy, anxiety, with nowhere to place it.

Maybe I needed more than the woods to escape. Gage had a woman now, Gunner the shooting range. Me? The only thing I had was an elusive whitetail that I didn't even have the balls to shoot.

What the *hell* was wrong with me?

I pushed into a jog, inhaling through my nose, exhaling through my mouth, maneuvering around rocks, jumping over logs. Faster, faster. It wasn't long before I felt like I was back in the military on a covert mission in the Wakhan Corridor of Afghanistan. It felt good.

God, I missed the military.

I pressed harder, sweat beading on my forehead. Faster, faster, faster, I sprinted through the rocky terrain in my T-shirt, khaki tactical pants, and ATAC boots. I could run in anything you could throw at me—a fact that was proven when my brothers dared me with a pair of six-inch platinum red heels... To this day, Gage wouldn't tell us where he'd gotten them, or more importantly, why he still had them. I couldn't walk for a week after, but I won that race. By a blister, but a win is a win nonetheless.

I looped back around to my ATV, slid behind the wheel, and took out my phone.

A picture of Erika Zajac filled the screen.

"Jesus *Christ,* man."

My head spun to see Gunner pulling up beside me. I hadn't even heard the guy coming and that was more alarming than seeing him outside of the shooting range.

"That's the second time I've caught you researching that chick in two days."

I closed out of the internet search I'd forgotten to click out of and slid my phone in my pocket. "What're you doing here? Ran out of targets?"

"I didn't realize you had the perimeter check tonight."

"Didn't realize you ever did it."

"I don't miss perimeter checks." Gunner narrowed his shaded eyes, looking me over. "She's a spoiled heiress to a finance empire, Ax, who'd recently broken up with some big shot banker on wall street, or had you not gotten to that article yet? Chick spends her shallow existence traveling the world on Daddy's money. You see her social media account?

She's like some rich-ass nomad without a single responsibility in the world."

I grunted, gripping the steering wheel. Yes, according to the multiple google searches I'd done on Erika Zajac since rescuing her from the cellar, Erika was the twenty-nine year old daughter of an immigrant who'd come to the states when he was five years old. At twenty-two her father hit big on a few tech stocks he'd invested in, then started his own private equity firm. At age thirty, Erika's dad had offices all over the country and was a multi-millionaire. He'd had four wives, and four high-profile divorces before kicking the bucket years ago. Erika's stepbrother inherited the company and was a frequent in the gossip columns. I'm pretty sure I even saw a picture of him walking a runway at some fashion show. Pussy. They were a blue blood family who spent their days in air-conditioned offices behind polished desks. The Zajac family was the picture of the elitist American dream, immigrants who'd moved to the US and struck gold by luck, so to speak, while the Steele family spent their days in the ditches, protecting the country that made their dream come true. Two very different perspectives. Two very different families.

And me and Erika? Two very different people. Erika was an impulsive free spirit who appeared to have no solid footing anywhere in her life. Me? My entire world ran on meticulously planned out schedules and paths. Spontaneity and I were like tequila shots and edible lube. Doesn't mix. Trust me on that.

Yep, Erika Zajac and Axel Steele were polar opposites on all counts.

And opposites do not attract.

Right?

Gunner continued, "But she is hot, I'll give her that. Have you talked to her?"

"Talked to her?" I said a little too defensively. "Like, call her up?"

"Whoa, man. Geez, yeah, like on the telephone?"

"No, I haven't seen or talked to her since the medics strapped her to the gurney and disappeared down Red Rock Trail."

"Have you heard anything about it? Who did it?"

"No. Just the headline on the news."

The story of two women being found chained to a cellar wall had made national news. It was a horrifying, salacious story that played to every woman's worst nightmare which made it an ideal story for the news. People couldn't get enough of the story. Sick bastards. Names of the victims had not been released at that point, which was interesting enough, and made me think it wasn't as simple as a former boyfriend snapping or something. The only way I knew Erika's last name was by coercing it out of one of my PD buddies after his third tequila shot. He'd also told me that authorities weren't even close to catching the son of a bitch who did it.

"Well, let it go, man." Gunner shrugged.

"Isn't that calling the kettle black."

We stared into the horizon, thinking of all the things we needed to let go.

And all the things we knew we'd die before doing so.

"Come on," he urged. "Jagg's on his way out. Says he needs to talk to us about something."

My brow tipped. Any time our buddy, former Navy SEAL turned state detective, said he "needed to talk to us," it usually wasn't about football.

I followed Gunner's ATV through the woods, scanning

our land as I passed through. Always on the lookout, always on alert. We picked up the trail and wound through the mountainside as the lampposts turned on, illuminating the long, paved driveway that snaked up our mountain to the compound. The main house came into view, an eight-thousand square-foot log and rock cabin with three floors, sweeping windows behind multiple decks, and intricate stone landscaping. The outdoor lights had turned on, shining onto the house and pine and oak trees that enclosed around it. The grandeur of it made us all a bit uncomfortable, but Dad liked nice things. Always had.

And at the top of the driveway, an unmarked black Cadillac Escalade.

Frowning, I pulled up next to Gunner, who'd stopped.

"You expecting someone?"

"Nope. I'm guessin' you aren't either."

My hand slid to the SIG on my hip. After a quick nod—the nonverbal communication my brothers and I were known for—Gunner pulled ahead and slipped into the woods. I kept my eyes on the vehicle as I topped the hill, just as Gage stepped onto the front porch.

Gage in front, me in the back, Gunner hidden and flanking from the east. One man down. We'd make do, as we always did.

I rolled to a stop behind the shiny, blacked-out vehicle and shoved the ATV into park, blocking it in. Brand-spanking-new, bullet proof windows and doors, V8, with tinted windows.

Our mystery guest was either famous, rich, or in a lot of trouble.

I didn't realize at the time I was about to get all three.

My head tilted to the side as I rounded the Escalade.

The door opened and a tank of a man unfolded himself

from the driver's seat. I grinned. Bald head slicked up with whatever lotion was on discount at the local grocery store. Black Ray-Bans, a blue golf shirt over, what, I'd guess, was two-hundred and thirty pounds of pure muscle, and pinched lips sure to intimidate any six year old. To top off the look, tattoos colored his hairless arms. Dude was the walking stereotype of a security detail wannabe. A former beat cop who got sick of working nights and decided to try his hand at private security in hopes of spending his days in close proximity to a thick pair of fake boobs and a thicker wallet.

He opened the back door as I walked up, fully aware of the amount of mud on my clothes, dirt in my beard, and sour scent of my pits. Luck of the unannounced visitor. Heed the warning.

"Mr. Steele..." A man slid out of the backseat and I recognized him instantly.

The odds... again...

He couldn't have been more than a handful of years older than I was—maybe just over forty—with coal-black hair slicked to the side without a single strand out of place. The light from the lampposts sparkled off a diamond-encrusted watch, which, somehow was less obnoxious than his navy pin-stripe suit, complete with a buttoned vest and printed tie. His skin was as smooth as a baby's ass and as tanned as a dairy cow. And if I had to guess, buffed to perfection to prevent the streaks from showing. Money, he wanted the world to know. Entitled pussy, I wanted him to know.

If a human being could be more opposite than I was, I was staring at him. And you want to know the funny thing? I bet my bank account could dance the Mexican Hat Dance around his.

I despised him the moment I laid eyes on him, and also, found myself scanning the back seat for his sister.

He extended his smooth hand and I caught the whiff of some fruity cologne, probably pressed in Italy and shipped in a sapphire box. "I'm—"

"I know who you are." I shook his hand. "Filip Zajac."

His eyebrow tipped ever so slightly. Yeah, no *Mr.* from me.

The opposite door opened and another man stepped out, this one mid-seventies with full head of silver hair pulled back into a pony tail. Same suit, different color, same watch, knock-off. While Filip carried the air of desperation for approval and admiration, this man didn't give a shit. Tall, muscular, confident.

I kept my eye on him.

"Yes, that's right, I'm Filip Zajac, CEO of Zajac Investments."

You're rich and you want me to take you seriously. Got it.

I stared back.

"And this is my business partner, Harrison Reid."

We shook hands, a strong, solid handshake. Unlike limp dick's. Harrison ran the show from the sidelines, no doubt about that.

Sensing the slightest undercurrent of tension, Gage stepped forward, stopping next to Rent-a-guard.

Filip continued. "First and foremost, thank you for saving my sister's life. I hope she repaid you somehow."

I nodded, but knew a face-to-face show of gratitude was not why this guy had shown up at my doorstep.

"How can I help you, Filip?"

"I'm in need of your services, Mr. Steele."

"Ax."

"Ax."

"You, personally?"

"Well, no."

"Which services then, exactly, Filip?"

"Personal security. You're the best."

"Media exaggerates."

"Detective Max Jagger strongly recommends your services."

I cut a glance at Gunner, whose subtle shift told me he had no clue what the guy was talking about.

He continued, "Regardless of Detective Jagger's recommendation, you've not only already saved my sister's life but your reputation proceeds you. I've heard you're the only Steele brother to lead multiple hostage rescue raids overseas. Says no one can stalk a target like you can."

My eyes narrowed to slits. The guy had been researching me and I didn't like it.

I didn't like it at all.

"I've been out of the military for a year," I said.

"It never leaves you." Harrison spoke, his voice deep.

Filip straightened, nodding at his business partner. "Before migrating to the states, Harrison was in the Polish Armed Forces."

I bit my tongue, then said, "I think you've misunderstood what we do here. We don't do recon work, and we aren't in search and rescue." I watched him closely, paying attention to his finger rolling over the edge of his thick, gold ring. The vein throbbing in his neck.

"I need the best, Ax. And that's you. My family, my business, has come under attack. I'm afraid that what happened to my sister is part of a bigger—"

He cut off as the rumble of an engine pulled my attention down the hill. Two headlights cut through twilight as a black Chevy Tahoe sped up the drive. I turned into the lights, and braced myself when it didn't slow. *Christ,* who invited Mario Andretti to the party? My head cocked, challenging the four-thousand pound missile on wheels as my hand slid next to my SIG. At a mere five feet from my body, the Tahoe turned and slid to a stop next to the Escalade. My interest in this impromptu visit now at its peak.

"And I need it now," Filip said the disdain deepening his sheltered voice as he eyed the other vehicle.

I eyed the Tahoe as well, now hidden behind the Escalade, crossing the hope that it might be his sister off my list because surely Erika drove a Maserati. Or maybe a bright red Ferrari. No, blue... blue to go with those eyes.

After catching Gunner's silhouette slip through the woods, flanking the newcomer, I shifted my attention back to Desperado. "We go through an extensive pre-authorization process before accepting new clients—"

"I'll pay double your fee."

"Filip—"

"Triple."

"Money isn't a motivator here."

"How about saving an innocent woman's life?"

I glanced toward the Tahoe again.

"Who exactly is in need of our services, Filip?"

The click of the car door opening pulled our attention. If attitude had a sound, it was defined in the slamming of that door.

My peripheral picked up Rent-a-guard moving toward what sounded like a five-hundred pound gorilla stomping across the gravel.

What I got was a five-foot-two inch hellcat with a platinum blonde braid cascading over her shoulder in a messy wave of shimmering silk, and a small yellow flower tucked behind one ear.

Time stood still as I watched every fantasy I'd had over the last four days walk toward me.

She wore a fitted T-shirt depicting a peace-sign giving Mona Lisa, the nun's two fingers a perfect *V* over one nipple of two very round breasts. My eyes drifted to the ink on her arms, more colorful, *more sexy*, now that the dirt and grime had been washed away. And topping off this juxtaposition of hippie and bad girl were ripped jeans and a pair of red joggers the color of her pillow-talking lips. And one hell of an annoyed expression on her pixie face.

I blinked.

Filip released an exasperated sigh. "Ax, I think you know my half sister, Erika Zajac."

8

AXEL

"*I* see you started without me." Erika's voice was strong, confident—*loaded*. The opposite of when I'd rescued her from the cellar. Her gaze shifted to me, endless lashes flickering above those spellbinding doe-shaped eyes, and I can honestly say I was speechless. For one second, I was completely, idiotically speechless.

"What part of stay on my bumper and don't get lost don't you understand?" Filip asked her in a condescending tone that should have earned him a slap in the face—a counterattack I would've loved to have delivered personally.

"The second part." Her baby blues shifted to Filip. "Considering I'm the topic of conversation, I assumed you'd wait. *Brother.*"

"I haven't even gotten to the details yet, *sister.*"

I was pulled from my stupor with a frown. It was like watching two elementary kids bicker on the playground. Not a good look.

Erika cocked her brow along with her curvy hip. "Oh, you mean trying to convince them that you're here solely to ensure your dear half sister is under the best protection possible, and not because you want to ensure your business doesn't get any more bad press? Remove the problem, remove the gossip. Isn't that right?"

Jesus.

I caught a glance from Gage, then from Gunner who'd made his way out of the woods and was enjoying both the view from Erika's backside, and the entertainment of the evening.

Filip shook his head, then turned his attention to me. "Well now that we're all here. Is there somewhere we can go to talk? I'm sure you'll accept Erika as a client after we lay out the details."

Truth was, I'd *accept* that smokeshow in the middle of a category five hurricane. But accepting her as a client was a totally different story.

I nodded at Gage, who turned and started into the house to alert the household of our guests. Gunner was busy giving Rent-a-guard a not-so-subtle once-over.

"Come on in," I said.

The blonde stunner stepped next to her brother and was met with a palm in her face.

"Erika, stay here with Mack."

Mack. Of course it was *Mack.*

She muttered something under her breath, and sensing another family squabble like stink on a pig, I glanced down and stepped back. Family squabbles in our house consisted of closed fists and busted lips. Thank God there were no female siblings, because arguing with a woman was something none of us were good at. Sure enough, a rapid-fire argument ensued and I wasn't surprised when Erika held her own against her bulldozing brother. He was at least a decade, maybe even fifteen years older than she was, and carried the same authority as a father-figure would. I watched her tip her chin up, a defiant gesture—and cute as hell, although I got the feeling she'd kick me in the balls if I told her that.

After another exasperated exhale, Filip pulled a folder from the Escalade then turned back to me as Erika followed Gage into the house.

"I'm sorry," he said, with Harrison close at his side. "She's... she's something else. Difficult. Defiant. Left home at sixteen, left dad, me, and went off on her own." We walked across the driveway. "We haven't even talked in years. She's a modern day gypsy... does as she pleases and doesn't know what's best for her, which is why I'm here. She's a sitting duck for what she's up against, if you ask me."

A hundred questions flooded my head at that moment, but I zeroed in on his last comment like a hawk.

"What do you mean, *what she's up against?*"

"You'll see."

We walked up the stone steps, with Gunner close behind. Obviously not invited to the party, Mack had taken a position leaning against the Tahoe, chatting on his phone. Another mistake for Renta. Cell phone use, for anything other than direct communication with my brothers, was strictly off-limits while guarding a client.

We crossed the covered entryway, then pushed through the wooden doors where Erika was gaping up at a painting that I'd recently purchased at a local art show. An autumn landscape full of light, magic, the colors leaping off the canvas with a vibrancy second only to the burning sun. Kind of like Erika.

"Beautiful home," Filip commented, pulling me back to attention. "How many acres do you guys have?"

"Three-thousand."

He nodded—as if this were an acceptable amount to

him—then he, Harrison, and Erika followed me down the hallway that ended at the conference room. Our home was broken up into living quarters—which was most of it—and business quarters, every room monitored by security cameras. We stepped into the conference room where Celeste, former Marine turned Steele Shadows Security office manager was opening the blinds, allowing the last of the setting sun to stream inside. Wearing her usual skinny jeans and flip flops, Celeste's long, black hair was down, running over a Steele Shadows Security T-shirt. The unlucky-in-love southern spitfire had two requirements when she'd signed on: Free access to our gun ranges anytime day or night, and no office attire. Both were granted on the spot. Over the years, Celeste had become the only woman, beside our stepmother, who could put us in our place and wrangle us when we needed it the most. She'd become invaluable to our business, knowing each of our clients personally, the dirtiest details of every case, dates, times, details like the back of her hand, and could recite every physical attribute of everyone she ever met. She was a walking file cabinet. And guys like us needed that.

The room filled with a golden glow of dusk emphasizing the rolling hills of the front lawn that faded into dense forests. It was a stunning view, which was intentional by our dad when he'd built the place. The view created a mixture of serenity and intimidation. A message of "we've got you" to our clients.

Filip sat in the middle of the table, Harrison next to him. Erika slid next to him. In a stark contrast to the serene view outside, Gunner had positioned himself at the back corner, wide stance, arms crossed over his chest. His usual stoic, statuesque self, which had intensified by a million percent since he'd stepped into Feen's shoes as unofficial CEO of Steele

Shadows Security. Gunner wasn't the best at meet-and-greets with prospective clients. Small-talking with the man was like trying to get a full sentence out of an orthognathic surgery patient who'd had their mouth sewn shut. Wasn't happening. But that was nothing compared to his lack of compromise. Gunner had a way of bulldozing people the moment they questioned his security tactics. It was Gunner's way or the highway, and that didn't make new clients feel all warm and fuzzy.

Gage leaned against the entryway, more relaxed, but just as alert.

"Would you like something to drink?" Celeste poured a glass of ice water, doing her best Emily Post.

"Please, thank you."

She passed out drinks as I made the introductions.

"Filip, this is Celeste Russo, our office manager." I turned to Celeste who had seated herself across from our three newcomers. "Celeste, this is Filip Zajac and his sister, Erika, and Harrison Reid." I sat at the head of the table. "Let's get started. What exactly brings you, both, here?"

Celeste flipped open her notebook.

Filip folded his hands on the table. "As I said, my sister's capture appears to be a part of a bigger thing, and it's my belief that she's still being targeted, as is my business."

"Still being targeted?"

He nodded. "Let me back up. Hours after Erika had disappeared, I received a ransom request for one million dollars—"

"How?"

"A phone call, to the direct line of the house. The police have determined it was a burner phone, untraceable."

"Did you recognize the voice?"

"No, they were using some sort of voice synthesizer."

I nodded for him to continue.

"I immediately began transferring assets when I received a call from the local PD that Erika had been found. That *you'd* found her."

I glanced at Erika. Her back as straight as a rod, she sat, staring at her hands folded on the table. Expressionless. Emotionless.

Concealed.

"Do you have the full police report?"

"Yes." Filip pulled several pieces of paper from his leather binder and slid it in front of me.

I scanned the paperwork, stopping cold on Erika's interview transcript. A ball formed in my gut as I read that she'd spent forty-eight hours in total darkness chained to that wall, fifteen feet underground. My pulse picked up as I flipped to her medical report—Erika had been severely dehydrated with bruised ribs, multiple contusions on her wrists and ankles where she'd tried to free herself from the cuffs, infected blisters on her fingertips, and a gash on her hip. Her emotional injuries were probably a whole other story. I cleared my throat and passed the papers to Celeste, then focused on the map that included the quadrants of the cellar. One-hundred and sixty-thousand acres of dense woods, Red Rock Park was a popular tourist destination. However, the cellar was located in a remote part of the park that was off-limits to hikers. Thanks to my own investigating, I'd learned the cellar had been part of an old log cabin that was torn down decades ago.

"Did security cameras pick up a vehicle in the area?" I asked.

"Plenty." Erika chimed in. "It's fall, a big tourist season for the park. They're in the process of running the plates."

I pointed at the map. "The cellar is within walking distance to, what looks like, a service road here."

"That's right. But there's plenty of access points, only blocked off by rusted chains. Plenty of alternative ways to get into the park."

"Are there cameras on that access road?"

"No. Trust me, I looked. He—"

"You looked?"

Her brow cocked. "Of course."

This woman was knee deep in her own investigation. Filip's words, *difficult, defiant,* flashed through my head.

She continued, "I believe our captor used either that service road or one of the surrounding access points, I'm sure of it."

Our captor. She was speaking of the other victim, the one who never made it out, and I wondered if she had some sort of survivor's guilt.

I shuffled through the papers. "I'm assuming the cellar has been swiped for prints, trace evidence? DNA?"

"Yes," Erika and Filip said simultaneously.

Filip slid her a look. "Everything collected has been sent off for analysis."

"Everything, and the other body." Erika said, the crack her in her voice confirming my guilt theory.

"Has the identity been—"

"Jessa Watson." Jagg breezed into the room. "Sorry I'm late. A twenty-nine year old socialite, heiress to her father's construction fortune. Her name was just released." He nodded at Filip, Erika and Harrison. "Good to see you all again."

Then, he cut me a glance that told me there was much more to this story. And I needed to know it. I turned back to Filip and Erika. "Tell me why you think Erika is a target."

"Because," Filip said quickly, "Last night, someone broke into her house."

Jagg shifted beside me.

"I wasn't there." Erika said. "But when I came home, the place was trashed. Someone broke in through the back door and wrecked the place."

"Was anything missing?"

"Jewelry."

"Do you have security cameras?"

She shook her head.

"But it has to be the same person." Filip insisted. "I mean, what are the odds?"

"So you think whoever did this is going to come after her again until he gets ransom money from you?"

"I do. I think it's best if she went away for a bit, stayed out of the public, off social media, off the radar until this guy is caught."

My gaze flickered to Erika, whose shoulders were as tense as Harrison's next to her.

"Erika," I said, "Do you believe that's the case?"

She shifted in her seat, her irritation evident. "I believe that my brother is afraid his money is at risk. But the police ruled that the break-in at my house wasn't related to what happened in the cellar. A done deal, in their books."

Jagg cleared his throat—and I received the message.

I glanced at Celeste. She flickered a nod of understanding, then stood. "Filip, Erika, Mr. Reid, can you please step over to the office with me for a moment?"

Gage closed the door behind them. Gunner pushed off the wall and met us at the head of the table.

"Talk," I said to Jagg.

"The FBI is working with state police on this—me, mainly—and here's what we know so far. Jessa Watson was kidnapped eight days ago from a bar after a night drinking with a few of her friends."

"From Berry Springs?"

"No, about twenty-five miles west from here. The street cameras show her abductor and her talking before she willingly got into the car."

"Meaning she knew him."

"Appears that way. Twenty-four hours later, her parents received an anonymous call requesting one million dollars be deposited in an account, threatening death if they didn't comply. The deadline was forty-eight hours. Well, turns out, The Watson's had seen their fair share of financial difficulties over the years and didn't have one-million bucks sitting in a savings account. They went to work gathering the money, selling shares of stock, whatever, but they couldn't come up with the cash in time. Twelve hours before the deadline, they were sent a video of their daughter, beaten, the whole nine yards. The deadline passed, and Jessa caught a bullet to the head. Her parents found out via a live video. Erika Zajac watched the whole thing. And by all counts, Erika had twenty-four hours left."

"But Erika wasn't an intended target. If her story is correct, she stumbled onto this nightmare."

"Right, and I believe that's true. I think whoever kidnapped Jessa saw Erika as an opportunity when he found out who she was through her cell phone."

"Filip mentioned you referred her to us."

Jagg nodded. "I don't believe the break-in at her home was random—"

"Unlike the police."

"Right. They sent a few items off to be scanned for DNA, which will take weeks, but they don't think there's enough evidence right now to connect the two incidents."

"But you do."

"Jessa Watson's autopsy was this morning." Jagg pulled his phone from his pocket, clicked into his images and held it up. A woman's thigh, multiple lacerations against bruised, grey skin illuminated the screen. He zoomed in. Below a brown mole was the letter *V* cut into the skin.

"The medical examiner almost missed it considering it's faded into the other lacerations. I didn't."

"And I'm guessing this isn't a love letter."

"Nope. *V* is the marking of the Black V's, a notorious gang quickly becoming one of the FBI's biggest headaches. It's their mark. I've been tracking these bastards locally for years."

I crossed my arms over my chest, not liking the turn this thing was taking. "I've heard of them. Originated in South America, been around for decades, big in drug trade."

"Not just any drug trade, they move some of the purest cocaine south of the boarder. Quality shit. Extremely expensive. They've grown substantially over the last five years, and eliminated their competition. The DEA estimates they own at least seventy percent of the cocaine market in Latin America."

"And by eliminating the competition, I'm assuming you don't mean they were provided severance packages."

"More like severed packages. These guys are brutal. They go beyond the stereotypical gang violence." He held up another picture, this one of a woman and children laying in front of a burning house with their eyes and tongues removed. "This woman's husband was suspected of turning over on a few of the members after he'd been arrested for third-degree assault. This was the gang's retaliation for ratting them out."

"Jesus."

"Not with these people. The Black V's have expanded their dealings becoming a multi-nation gang. They're ruthless. Anyone who rats them out or turns against them is viciously murdered, tortured, the works."

"And this doesn't bode well for Erika Zajac."

"Exactly. And it's not only that Erika single-handedly witnessed one of their killings, it's that Erika *got away*. Thanks to you, Ax. Whoever killed Jessa and held Erika captive now has a bounty on his head by the rest of the gang, unless he finds and eliminates her as a threat. Think about it. To them, she's a walking rat."

"*Shit,*" Gunner muttered as he ran his fingers through his hair.

Jagg shifted his attention to Gage. "Mickey Greco, the foster parent of the dude who went after your girl, Niki, a few weeks ago? There's an email trail linking him to them. We think he was trying to get into bed with the Black V's."

Gage's fists clenched at his sides. This thing was already hitting close to home.

"That cellar has got to be a treasure trove of DNA evidence... even his hair, anything. Why hasn't the guy been caught?"

"Takes time. The crime scene team is still filtering through the dirt, looking for anything that can lead them to this guy."

"So, hold on." I held up a hand. "The FBI's on this. Why isn't Erika in protective custody?"

"Again, not enough to link the break-in at her house to the incident in the cellar."

"Bullshit," I snapped.

Jagg held his hands up—*I know.*

I began pacing. "How close is the FBI to nailing him?"

"You mean the one after Erika specifically?"

"Sure."

Jagg laughed. "They're after the big fish, Ax. They wanted the leader of the Black V's. You know how that goes."

"And how close are they to finding the big fish?"

Jagg held up his phone again.

"Recognize him?"

"Senator Inglewood."

"Yep. Asshole's currently under secret surveillance by the FBI for suspected interaction with the V's."

"You're kidding."

"Nope, this thing had legs. Tentacles. And we think it goes way beyond red bandanas, ripped jeans, and tattoos. We think the V's have infiltrated some of the most elite circles in our country, including politicians. We think they're embedded into some of the richest circles in the country."

"Using the cocaine?"

"That's how they get in the door, yeah."

"Does the FBI think Senator Inglewood is *part* of the Black V's? An actual member?"

"It's an angle they're pursuing. Inglewood and many others, including CEO's of fortune five-hundred companies."

"No *shit?*"

"Nope."

My mind spun. "Ransom, Senators, CEO's... the connection is money. Greed. One of the seven deadly sins. Money is the root of all evil—and the downfall. It's a weakness. Easy to exploit."

"For the Black V's, yes. But that's not why I recommended Filip bring Erika here." Jagg's narrowed eyes focused on me. "The person who's hunting Erika doesn't care about money, Ax, the person hunting Erika cares about his life. If he doesn't get Erika, the Black V's will not only kill him, but his entire family. He's a weak link."

My gut clenched.

"Ax, this man will hunt Erika until his last breath, because if he doesn't, the Black V's will take it from him. You're up against someone with everything to lose."

My hands curled to fists.

If the last two weeks had proven anything to me, it was that the will to live was the strongest power on earth.

And Erika Zajac was in a heap of trouble.

9

AXEL

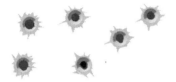

I glanced out the windows to the four silhouettes outlined against the glow of the lampposts. Celeste, Filip, Harrison, and Erika. The mistress of my dreams the last four days. Stealer of my nights. The lean legs underneath a worn pair of Levi's that seemed a mile long despite her small frame. Curvy hips marked by an hourglass waist. And that hair, a mess of white gold hypnotizing me into an insta-fantasy where I ripped the hair tie from the bottom of that tangled braid, cupped the back of her head, and—

Jesus.

Jagg's voice faded to nothing but a murmur as I watched her for a moment as she gazed out at the mountains, fixed on the last sliver of light sitting on the horizon. She stood strong, tall, shoulders back, controlled, except for the fists she held at those rounded hips. It was the only indication of emotion other than that fiery attitude she wore with no apologies. That much was obvious. Hell on earth as a young, inquisitive child. Hell on earth as a client.

My gaze shifted to her brother Filip, and his business

partner, Harrison Reid, stepping onto the lawn with Celeste at their side. Giving a quick tour, I imagined.

There was something behind that childish rivalry between Erika and her brother that I couldn't quite put my finger on. I didn't like that. What also bothered me was the fact that it was as obvious as a train wreck that Erika didn't think she needed our services—that, or, she felt like she could handle things on her own. She also didn't come across as someone who did whatever people told her to do.

So, why was she there?

Why did she agree to come with her brother—someone she obviously couldn't stand—and seek our services?

Things weren't adding up and I knew I wasn't getting the full picture, from him *or* her, and I didn't like that one bit.

I looked back at Erika, who had pulled away from the group, close enough to hear the conversation, but far enough to make sure everyone knew she didn't give two shits. Far enough to make her over-protective brother keep a bead on her, his attention flickering to her every few seconds. And with every flicker, Erika moved exactly two feet farther away.

Rich girl problems.

Filip said something to her, and she obliged him with a quick nod, followed by a few more steps separation. Following the landscape, Erika turned, her profile outlined with her silhouette. Rogue strands of hair danced across her face, catching in the breeze. Eyes narrowed, she focused on the driveway, her tongue darted across her lips, stealing my focus for the third time that evening. Her chin lifted, jaw clenched as she scanned the mountains... looking for something.

Someone.

One thing that had stood out to me was that this woman

wasn't cowering behind her rich brother, or Rent-a-guard, for that matter. Not that that would have helped matters. No, if anything, the look on Erika Zajac's face at that moment was fearless, resolute.

Determined.

And fearless, resolute, determined was not the norm for a woman seeking our services.

Fearless was worst-case scenario.

Steele Shadows had taken on several socialites over the years, the threat ranging from obsessed ex-boyfriend, to serial killers. The cases were different, sure, but the women were all the same—spoiled, rich kid brats who couldn't make a sound decision to save their lives. The little world their parents had created around them was theirs to rule, everyone else be damned. Hard work was as foreign to them as the half-off section in a discount grocery store. To them, material things were as vital to life as low cholesterol and oxygen.

Entitlement.

Nothing sickened me more than entitled assholes.

Absolutely nothing made me want to walk away from a case more.

Erika turned, and like a magnet, pinned me through the windows.

And goddammit if my heart didn't give a little kick.

"Ax?"

I tore my eyes away. "Sorry, what?"

Jagg flickered a glance to Erika before focusing back on me. The detective didn't miss a thing. "I was saying, my gut's telling me that this girl's in a heap of trouble... but that she's also an asset."

"An asset?"

He nodded. "She's the witness to a cold-blooded Black V murder. Her testimony could unravel the group."

"If she stays alive."

"If she helps catch the guy who did it."

"Where're you going with this, Jagg?"

"Erika Zajac is the only one to live through a brutal meeting with the V's. The only one to see one and stay alive to talk about it."

"Wait. The police report says she said she never got a clear picture of the guy. Never saw his face."

"*Voices*, Ax, she heard his voice. Not only that, she could have registered more than she even realizes. Hell, you know all about that. A rescued victim who'd been under duress for days might not be able to recall a single thing until they come across some sort of trigger. Something that jogs their memory. Ax, Erika could be the catalyst to bring down an entire gang."

"So, what the hell? You're wanting me to take her back to the cellar? See what she remembers? What?"

Jagg reached into his pocket and handed me a piece of paper. Under bright colors of yellow, orange, and brown were the words *Fall Harvest Gala*. A few lines underneath that read *Senator Inglewood invites you...*

Dread pooled in my gut. "You're fucking kidding me."

Gunner yanked the paper from my hands. "It's dangling a piece of meat, dude."

A rush of anger flushed my cheeks. I closed the inches between the detective, my friend, and tipped up my chin. "You're wanting to use her as *bait.*"

Jagg mirrored my rigid stance with one of his own. A former Navy SEAL, the man never backed down from a fight, and had the scars to prove it.

"Relax, Ax." His voice calm, deep, and laced with warning. "I'm saying it's an opportunity to jog her memory. To move the case along. To help nail down a dangerous group of assholes who're only getting bigger by the day. Yeah, there's a chance members of the Black V will be there. That's the entire point. It's an opportunity too great to pass up."

"At the potential cost of her life."

He cocked his head. "Your confidence is slipping, Ax. She'd be under *your* security."

"Your calculated manipulation doesn't work on this Steele brother, Jagg. *You're* slipping."

Jagg stepped back. "I get it, Ax. What I don't get is what Jessa Watson's family is going through. What countless others are, at the hands of the V's. That's *my* job, Ax. To help find these sons of bitches and bring them to justice. To help get closure for the families that haven't even begun to heal. I know you understand that... especially right now, Axel."

I glanced down, my thoughts instantly consumed by Phoenix. What would Feen do? If he was there, what would Phoenix do? My ruthless older brother would do whatever the hell he needed to do to catch a killer.

"Does Erika even know all this? Does she know about the Black V's?"

"No. She and her brother know the same limited information, only. She knows that this is part of a bigger thing, thanks to the FBI's interviews with her. She knows there are other related homicides, and she's picked up that Senator Inglewood might somehow be involved. That's it. Her brother and I are the ones that convinced her to come here."

"What convincing did you have to do?" I asked before I could catch myself. Max Jagger was known as much for his rugged good-looks and intricate tattoo work as he was for his infallible instinct at a crime scene. Women dropped to their knees in front of him and I assumed Erika had been no different. More importantly, why did I even care?

Jagg snorted. "I'd be lying if I didn't think about it, but that woman is way too rich for my blood. Never was one for spoiled rich girls. Little too wily, too."

"What about Rent-a-guard?" Gage asked. "Can't he handle this shit?"

Jagg shook his head. "Filip hired him from some hole-in-the-wall security firm an hour after he got the ransom phone call. No, that dude cannot handle the Black V's. Steele Shadows?" He put his hand on my shoulder. "Probably their only worthy adversary."

"Gentlemen?" Celeste cut us off with a pained tone as if it took every ounce of her pride to address us professionally. Filip and Harrison followed her into the room, with Erika lingering in the entryway. Brow tipped, Celeste looked back and forth between Jagg and I indicating that she wanted to move this little visit along. Patience was never one of Celeste's strong suits, especially where there was a playoff game on TV.

"Just a second. There's one more thing," Filip said, eyeing Gunner and me.

God*damn* one more things.

"I want Mack to stay with her, too."

"Absolutely not."—*"No."*—"No way." Gage, Gunner, and I said simultaneously.

"I've paid for his services for a month."

"If you feel like Erika needs an additional layer of service we can lay out some more options for you, or you can take your business elsewhere, but your bodyguard will not be staying on our grounds."

Filip narrowed his eyes, his patience waning, too. "Fine. He'll be available if needed, then." Filip checked his watch. "Let's move this along. Will you accept Erika or not?"

"He will." Jagg said, ushering Filip and Harrison to the doorway before I could knee him in the balls.

I turned to Gunner, who said, "Something's weird here. Off. Someone's not telling us something."

"Agreed. Let's find out what we can about Filip, Renta, Harrison—"

"You think her brother ordered a hit on his own sister?"

"Half sister, and I'm not saying that. Just that we need to look at everything here."

Gunner nodded, as deep in thought as I was.

"And Filip's company, too. Zajac Investments."

He cocked his brow. "A Fortune 500 finance company with an owner who likes shiny things..."

"Exactly."

My peripheral caught Erika striding across the foyer.

Gunner leaned in. "I don't like this one, Ax. Keep your head on a swivel."

He breezed past her as she stepped into the room like a tornado. Eyes locked on me, she said, "Can I have a moment, please."

I dipped my chin in agreement, staring down at the deep blue specks hidden in her irises.

"My brother likes to run the show, always has, and I like to let him think he does. But we both know that this is my decision. I'll become your client under one condition, Mr. Steele."

She was the opposite of the person who wrote me the sweet, heartfelt letter. Maybe she regretted it. Hell, maybe she'd decided she didn't care much for me after spending a few minutes with me. I stared down at her, at this erratic woman who seemed to change the game with every play.

And then, she did.

"I'm going to that party tonight."

My gaze sliced Jagg who was eyeing me from the foyer. Unbelievable.

"What party?" I asked, buying some time while my thoughts spun.

"The Fall Harvest Gala."

I grit my teeth, willing fire to shoot out of my eyes and singe Jagg's abnormally long arm hair.

"Well?"

"Miss Zajac, under the circumstances—"

"Under the circumstances, it is a good bet Jessa's killer will be at that party."

Survivors guilt. Dammit.

She continued, "He'll be there, I know it."

"All the more reason to stay away, don't you think?"

"Not if I recognize him. Not if I can point him out."

I glimpsed over her shoulder where Gunner and Celeste were pretending to not be listening.

She clicked her tongue demanding my attention back on her.

It worked.

"I'm doing this with or without you, Axel."

And she would. I saw the determination. This woman was on a one-way mission to thwart any plans to stay out of the public, *and* danger.

Her perfectly pointed eyebrow tipped up.

She was challenging me and I got the vibe that most men she challenged were quick to bend over for her.

Jesus. *Christ.*

"Axel—

"Ax."

"Ax... I'm going, whether—"

"You go to this party on your own, you can forget about our security."

"I understand, which is why I'm asking you. Listen," she shifted her weight. "I believe there's still a threat, yes, and I believe that the break-in at my house was connected to the cellar. I understand why I'm here—despite what you think."

"It's a logistical nightmare, Ax" Gunner muttered from the doorway, to which Erika coolly responded—

"So will my funeral be."

I clenched my jaw.

She continued, "I can help get this guy before he takes another victim."

I glowered down at her, the ball in my gut tightening. No, Erika wouldn't help keep another potential victim safe.

Because she was the next victim.

I pushed past her. "Celeste," I forced out against all better judgement. "Book her."

Celeste nodded and stepped into the foyer.

"What time's the blessed party?" I muttered as I breezed past Jagg and started up the staircase.

"Two hours."

"Celeste. Tell Erika I'll pick her up in ten minutes."

"For what?"

"Self-defense."

"Ax, wait, come on, she just got here—"

"Which one, Celeste?"

"... Cabin 2."

10

ERIKA

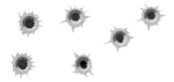

I had just enough time to change clothes before Ax showed up at the door of what was apparently Cabin 2. After my brother had left, satisfied that I was tucked away somewhere, Celeste had escorted me down a landscaped, lighted path through the woods to a small row of cabins barely visible through the dense trees. I was surprised at how quaint they were. I'd expected a tin building surrounded in booby-traps and trip wire, what I got was warm and welcoming.

Well, with everything except my new bodyguard.

After walking me through a security system that involved a remote control with more buttons than a computer, a unique security pin, and an *SOS* necklace, Celeste left with a warning that Ax was extremely punctual, and a look that told me I'd better hustle.

She knew her team well.

Another knock—*bang,* more like—then Ax disappeared back into his ATV, impatiently awaiting my presence. To take a *self-defense* course. What the heck? I was familiar with the Steele brothers' reputation for not coddling their clients.

They took their job very seriously, and according to Celeste, my protection would be their number one priority. That was good—no arguments there, but to throw me into a self-defense course ten minutes after I'd signed on the dotted line seemed a bit extreme.

Could a woman get settled first?

Was a drink too much to ask?

I slid a light jacket over my pink tank top and yoga shorts—because what do you wear to a self-defense class?—and cursed myself when I took a second to check the mirror and smooth the braid that ran over my shoulder.

Ax didn't even flicker a glance at me when I got into the ATV. He was irritated and not bothering to hide it. Was it me? My brother? Was this his actual personality? So different than the knight in shining armor days before? What had him so pissed?

Sure, I demanded to attend a party that evening.

Yeah, I'd made a deal.

Fine, an ultimatum.

But surely it wasn't the first time a woman had stood up to the guy, had given him options that he had to choose from. Although, meeting him now, all smooth bad boy swagger with eyes that could melt a glacier, maybe the options only involved 'my bed or yours.' It bothered me that I hadn't heard back from him after I sent the card. Why, I wasn't really sure, but I figured I'd get at least a thank you. Maybe I *wanted* to talk to him again, maybe even see him again. But I hadn't anticipated how much it would upset me when he didn't mention it now that we were face to face. Nothing. Not a word.

Perhaps he'd never received it. Perhaps he thought it was stupid.

Perhaps the stone that meant so much to me was in the bottom of a ravine somewhere.

It embarrassed me, to be honest, that he hadn't mentioned it. Like I'd put a piece of my heart out there, and had already been denied. And so I told myself I wouldn't bring it up, unless he did. And I'd try to move on.

But I knew I'd never forget it—the moment Axel Steele kneeled down in front of me in that cellar, all shadows and fate, with eyes that promised more than just my freedom. Something had stirred deep inside me.

The guy looked like he'd been in a war zone, with dirt, grime, and God knew what else painted on his face, dead leaves sprinkled in his hair, a crossbow dangling from a pack that was almost invisible against his clothes. He was massive with thick, broad shoulders and cannons for arms and legs, and at that moment, he was as much beast as man. Through the muck, though, those bright green eyes shone like emeralds, feral almost, pinning me more than the chains on my arms and legs. I'll never, ever forget that moment.

It wasn't until the next day I'd learned that the man who saved me was Axel Steele, billionaire former spec ops Marine turned businessman. Basically every woman's wet dream.

I thought I'd never see him again.

Until fate intervened and unveiled an opportunity too good to pass up. One that would have Axel kicking me to the curb if he knew about.

The Steele brothers weren't what I expected, which was a bunch of older men in black suits with ray-bans and shiny new Gs hidden under their jackets. No, what I got was a trio of thirty-something, jacked-up former military dudes with enough testosterone to empty a convent, and enough sex appeal to turn heads at an LGBT convention. They were the walking definition of ruggedly handsome, with tanned skin, calloused hands from hours of manual labor, and an inherently steely look that had a way of making you feel an inch tall—and an intensity that made you want to be on the receiving end of whatever they kept so pent up inside.

But something about Ax was different, though.

Unlike his brothers, there was a hyper-awareness behind those eyes, like a calculator going on overdrive in his head. His brothers seemed the type to snap at any minute, destroying everyone and everything in their paths. Not Ax. No, Ax would be the one devising the getaway plan in the background.

It was interesting watching "Business Ax" versus "Hero Ax," sitting at the head of a boardroom table, weighing if I was worthy enough of his services. There was an authority that oozed from the guy. A self-confidence as subtle as a nuclear bomb, a self-assurance that made everyone in the room watch him and do exactly as he said. He didn't boast, flex his muscles, bulldoze a conversation, raise his voice, no that simply wasn't Ax.

You know the kind of guys that 'demand respect?' That wasn't Ax either.

Respect came easily to him.

Innately.

By only entering the room. It was as simple as that from him. I wondered what it would be like to have that kind of confidence, that kind of effect on people. God, the things I could do. Or better yet, the things I could control.

The Steele brothers were all alpha, no doubt about that, and all skilled in saving the damsel in distress, and if I had to guess, had plenty. Shredded alpha males who'd spent their lives fighting bad guys and protecting women. Walking commitment-phobes. Walking ladies' men.

Walking aphrodisiacs.

If you liked that sort of thing.

Me? I fell hard for it, face first into a puddle of my own desperation.

Which was exactly why I needed to keep my eye on the ball, and off Ax's perfectly formed ass.

Ax was smooth, adaptable—which he'd proven with how he dealt with my brother, the only sign of his annoyance was the occasional twitch of his jaw. I could see why Ax ran the show. That guy didn't miss a thing. He was the smooth one.

The manipulative one.

And this told me that I needed to be careful with him, because I had other things on my mind than staying out of trouble.

In fact, my plans involved that very thing.

We drove past an Olympic sized swimming pool, a patio complete with its own kitchen and flat-screen TV's. Past a basketball courts, tennis courts, and two MMA-looking fighter cages. All lit up against the growing darkness.

It was a bachelor pad on steroids.

Correction: *Billionaire* bachelor pad on steroids.

Deep orange faded into a dark sky where stars were just beginning to twinkle. Steele Shadows Security was out in the middle of nowhere, deep in the Ozark mountains, all a sparkling color of yellow, orange, and red under outdoor lighting. It was amazing.

I'd heard they'd rarely left their compound, and now, I had a good idea why.

Ax rolled to a stop under a tree, cut the engine and got out.

I guessed I was supposed to follow. I also guessed this dismissive attitude toward me was going to get on my nerves —quickly.

"Indoor or outdoor?"

I studied the large metal building with no windows, then the caged wrestling ring next to it.

"They both look miserable."

"Indoor it is."

He stepped in front of me and pushed through a thick metal door, where I was assaulted with screaming rock music and that sour scent of "gym."

"Whoa." I looked around the massive room, an endless concrete floor speckled with wrestling rings, free weights, a torture-chamber-looking obstacle course, and machines that would rival any upper east side New York City gym. Three guys built like tanks were working out. My attention was pulled to a *'fuck you'* in the corner where two guys wearing nothing but spandex were engaged in hand to hand combat. No helmet, no pads, no gloves, just bright blue mouth pieces.

Gotta protect those teeth. Brain not so much, teeth, a must.

"Towels there, water there." Ax nodded to a rack against the wall as he clicked down the blaring music on a panel of flashing buttons and screens that showed various views of the gym, inside and out. The harsh metal building resembled an old garage from the outside, but had all the bells and whistles of a spaceship on the inside. And I wondered if that were on purpose.

It became clear to me that the Steele brothers spared no expense. On anything.

Ax breezed by me and walked to the ring where the animals were fighting. Again, I followed. We watched for a while, the two men unaware of our presence. Both were shredded—Men's magazine shredded—and somewhere north of six-foot. One, dark, shaggy hair and mean-looking tattoos all over his body, the other clean shaven, tan, and glistening in sweat.

I felt my pulse start to pick up watching them. I never did like fighting. It always unsettled me, made me a bit sick to my stomach. And considering my past, that wasn't an unexpected reaction.

"Who are these guys?" I asked as one slammed a knee into the other's gut.

"Part of our team."

"Of Steele Shadows Security?"

A quick nod.

"They're bodyguards?"

"Yep."

"Wow. I didn't realize you had so many employees. You all find work here in Berry Springs?"

"No. We train here, mostly, then they're sent to one of our offices around the country."

"How many offices do you have?"

"A few. Wolf," Ax yelled over the music, signaling to me that our conversation was over.

The tanned one glanced over, and the tattooed one surprised him with a right hook. Then, fighting again.

Ax shook his head. *"Wolf."*

Tattoo pinned Ken-doll, then finally noticed us standing there. "Well hey there boss." Tattoo sauntered over, his eyes never leaving my body. "New one?"

My brows tipped.

"Yep—"

"Erika—"

Ax and I said simultaneously.

"This is Wolf," Ax nodded to tattoo-guy. "Head of security. Wolf, this is Erika Zajac, a new client in Cabin 2."

"Good cabin."

Um, okay? He skimmed my body, pausing on my tattoos. Amped up testosterone, I assumed, or maybe a total ladies' man like everyone else around here, but the dude was metaphorically undressing me.

"We're starting out with self-defense." Ax said, shifting closer to me.

"Ah, well, you've come to the right place." Wolf finally looked at Ax. "Where do you want us?"

"Wait..." I turned to Ax. "I thought... are you not..."

"Wolf is one of the best self-defense teachers around."

I looked at the mat, now vacant. Ken doll had toweled off and was making his way to the free weights.

"What's the matter? Afraid of a little sweat?" Wolf grabbed a towel and began wiping himself down. "Fine, I'll clean off and might even put in a breath mint for you." He winked.

"You're too kind." Nerves zipped through my stomach.

"Watch her wrists and ankles," Ax said to Wolf.

"They're fine." I said.

"Alright," Ax nodded to the mat. "Let's go, sweetheart." He lifted the padded rails for me.

"You call me sweetheart again and I might show you exactly how much self-defense I already know." I slid under the rail.

Wolf laughed then wiggled his eyebrows at Ax, who didn't look amused. God, that guy.

My bodyguard stood on the sidelines, his face hard, body rigid, arms crossed over his chest, fully focused on us as a coach would his team. It made me uncomfortable, like he was judging me.

And for some reason, I had absolutely no doubt that he was.

"Lesson one. "Keep your focus at all times. Got it?" Wolf said as I peeked again at Ax and watched him watch Wolf. "Never get distracted."

My head snapped toward a loud *boom* across the room, and before I could register what was happening, my feet flew out from under me in response to the full body slam I'd just been delivered. The breath knocked out of my lungs as I slammed against the mat, a heavy body against mine. My head was still spinning when Wolf pushed off me and jumped up.

"What the *hell* was that?" I blinked, turned my head to a snickering Ken-doll in the corner, then glowered up at the body towering over me.

Wolf put his hands on his hips. "Never get distracted, Erika. I was standing right in front of you, literally telling you to focus, in the middle of a ring where the entire purpose is the fight. You knew you were here for self-defense training, you knew something was coming, and not only that, I'm a total stranger. Why trust me? One little sound and you lost focus. Looked away, and got your ass handed to you."

With a huff—and glare shot at Ax—I pushed to my feet.

"In any scenario, especially one that's new, always keep your focus. When you're jogging, hiking, in the parking lot, walking from building to building, full focus on the current moment, all the time. No cell phone, nothing. Do I have your full focus now, Miss Zajac?"

"Erika. And undivided." I narrowed my eyes and shifted to the balls of my feet.

"Good. Okay, let's begin. Always remember, you have

multiple deadly weapons on you at all times. You are never without a weapon. You, Erika, are lethal."

I smirked.

"I'm not being funny. Think of your body as a weapon. Your hands, arms, legs, feet, mouth, teeth, every single part of you can be used in some way to kill your attacker. You *are* strong. Women power, right?"

I tilted my head to the side. "Why'd you grin when you said that?"

"Just trying to get you pissed at me."

"We're beyond pissed at this point."

"Good. Use that, and use your body. Okay?"

I nodded, the butterflies in my stomach now a flock of birds. I fought stealing another look at Ax. Damn that man. *He* was stealing my focus.

Wolf rubbed his hands together and stretched his neck. "Okay, first we'll start with the most common scenario." He walked around me. "Stay."

I froze.

He disappeared behind my back. "Let's say you've forgotten your focus lesson and you're chatting away on your cell phone like an idiot while walking to your car, or you're zoned out on your jog listening to the latest self-help podcast—"

"Because only women listen to self-help podcasts?"

"You said it, not me. Anyway, you've let your mind drift. He sees that, and he takes advantage."

Two tattooed cannons wrapped around my torso and pinned down my arms. "Now, I've got you pretty good, don't I?"

He did, and it was terrifying.

"The key here is to use what you have. When you're bear hugged from behind, drop your weight."

"Okay..."

"... Now, Erika."

"Oh, uh right now?"

"*Yes,* right now. Bend your knees and drop your weight. Your goal here is to become more difficult for me to handle, to move, to carry away. Bend your knees, drop your ass, and wiggle. Thrash around."

I did as instructed and sure enough, I felt his grip begin to weaken.

"Now, go for my balls. Kick your heel up."

I threw back my heel and was released.

I turned. Wolf smiled. "Woulda got me. Nice work."

"Thanks," I squeaked, the adrenaline starting to amp me up.

"Stay there." He moved behind me again and wrapped his arm around my neck.

"Scary, huh?"

I tried to nod, but my head was locked.

"Again, focus. Don't let fear overcome you. What weapon do you have right now that you can use?"

"My hands," I ground out.

"Nice. *Exactly.* Imagine your own hands—your weapons —as iron hooks, grabbing and ripping mine down, away from you. Are you ready?"

His grip began to tighten around my neck, and my chest began to tighten. I peeked at Ax, the muscles in his jaw clenched, squinting with more than just focus.

"Yes."

"Okay, go."

As he squeezed around me, I dropped my weight and began ripping at his hands, his grip around my neck loosening. He released and stepped back.

"Good work."

My heart a steady pounding, we worked through a few other behind-the-back scenarios and I noticed Ax had begun pacing, like a tiger outside of the cage. Watching Wolf and I with a ferocity that pulled my focus more times than I cared to admit. To Wolf, anyway.

"Now, lie down."

Chest heaving and sweaty now, I cocked my head. "Lie down?"

"This is self-defense not a porno." Wolf tilted his head to meet mine. "Although that doesn't sound half bad right about now."

A low grunt from beside the ring.

Wolf grinned, keeping his eyes on me. "Down."

I lowered to the mat.

"*All* the way down."

My peripheral vision caught Ax's pacing increasing, back and forth, faster and faster. As I lowered to my back, I glanced over. His focus was on Wolf now, not me. Wolf either didn't notice or didn't care as he straddled me. I tried to pay attention to what he was saying, but began to feel the heat rise to my cheeks as his groin pressed against mine. With Ax watching from the sidelines, it felt like the prologue to some erotic threesome.

My heart started to race as Wolf leaned down saying something about my body being a weapon again.

I turned my head, searching for Ax, who'd disappeared. Just then, a flash from the side, then Wolf was catapulted off me, his body flying through the air. I gasped, lifted and watched Wolf and Ax tumble to the ground, fists flying, legs kicking. But that was short-lived by Ax pinning him, his hands around his head of security's throat. The hostile, feral look in Ax's eyes sent a chill up my spine as he looked over at me and said—

"Above all else," his voice gravelly, terrifying. "Always know your surroundings."

Wolf heaved Ax off him with a grin, then cocked his brow. "Think we're done here, Miss Zajac."

Ignoring him, Ax stalked over and with irritated, jerky movements, helped me off the mat, never looking into my eyes. I didn't know what to say.

Wolf chuckled as he walked away.

"Go get ready for your party," Ax grumbled as he tossed me a towel and stepped out of the ring, still avoiding eye contact. "I'll pick you up in thirty."

"But I don't know my way back—"

Without turning around, he said, "Celeste will take care of it."

I watched Ax blow out of the building as Celeste stepped inside, wondering what the heck just happened.

11

ERIKA

*B*utterflies tickled my stomach as I twisted my hair into a loose bun on the top of my head. I didn't have the time or patience to straighten the wavy, frizzed-out mess it had become after my little self-defense course. So I'd added a few small braids on the side and pulled it up. I slid on a pair of earrings, smoothed my red lip gloss and stepped back to gauge my efforts.

The makeup had done a solid job of covering the dark circles under my eyes and fading bruise on my chin from when I'd fallen on the cellar floor. I'd packed a long curve-hugging, long-sleeved, gunmetal gray dress to conceal the marks on my wrists and ankles, paired with black six-inch heels.

Gunmetal gray to fit the mood I felt inside.

Backless to remind everyone I could hold my damn own.

I glanced at the clock—7:04pm.

Twenty minutes.

I snorted. I didn't need twenty minutes to get ready. Never did. No, that kind of self-absorbed behavior went to my mother and stepmothers. All three of them. Twenty minutes was the amount of time it took to apply a single fake eyelash. Growing up, the prepping and primping that went on behind closed doors at the Zajac estate took hours upon hours, and multiple staff members, while I was hidden away in my room, covered in a rainbow of colors, doing the only thing that ever made me feel... *me.*

I inhaled deeply, then exhaled, trying to rein in the anxiety that was creeping up. I grabbed my Chanel handbag and stepped into the living room of Cabin 2.

I studied the paintings that hung on the thick log walls, all nature, but not redneck I-love-to-hunt pictures. No, these were beautifully painted landscapes, each pulling you into a moment, an artist's vision so thoughtfully executed that you felt like you were there. Or, wanted nothing else in the world than to be there. I was drawn to one of a sunrise, so bright with promise and hope of a new day. No name at the bottom, and I made a mental note to ask Celeste. I reached up and traced my finger along the sunbeams, marked by two bluebirds against the rays of light. My stomach dropped.

With a knot in my throat, I turned away and walked mindlessly around the living room, tracing my fingers along the walls, fighting the memories that were threatening to paralyze me with every passing minute. The memories I'd tried so hard to push aside the last thirteen years.

Another deep breath as I looked around the cabin, all neutral colors, warm and earthy, bringing the outdoors inside. The floors were polished oak, running underneath brown leather sofas and woven rugs. A bedroom and marble bathroom flanked either side of a massive stone fireplace, the focal point of the space. I'd spotted the treadmill tucked in the corner of the bedroom and thanked my lucky stars for that. At least one thing I could do to release energy while being cooped up. Copper cookware speckled a small granite kitchen with a breakfast nook in the corner. But hands down, my favorite part was the floor-to-ceiling windows that led to a deck that overlooked the mountains. I'd already decided on a morning yoga session out there.

I looked at the clock again—more butterflies, so I made my way into the kitchen and found a nice bottle of red above the fridge. Truth was, I would have taken a sip of moonshine at that moment to calm the nerves flowing through my system. I poured, sipped and leaned against the counter, wondering how long I'd be banished to the mountains of Berry Springs. Call it psychic, call it a woman's intuition— which some would say was psychic—but I knew he was going to be at that party. I always knew we would see each other again. And hopefully, the bastard would be locked up by the time the last bottle of cheap Brut was popped, and I'd be on my way home.

A thirteen year victory.

I took a deep sip and focused on the stars just beginning to twinkle in the sky.

Like a trailer on loop, the memories crept into my head, as they had done every hour for the last six days.

"911, what's your emergency?"

I blinked, frozen in a state of paralyzing shock as I stood at the top of the alleyway, the piss-yellow glow of the busted streetlight pooling over her body next to the dumpster, her blue dress now saturated with blood.

"Hello? 911, what's your emergency?"

"I need help," the words came out in a breathless whisper.

"They killed her. They killed her. I need help. She's dead." The phone tumbled to the ground as the world spun around me.

"They killed—"

Lights reflected off the walls, pulling me out of my nightmare. I blinked the tears away, took another gulp of wine and cleared my throat. A low grumble cut through the silence as a blacked-out Chevy pulled to a stop next to the porch and cut the engine.

Six minutes early. I shouldn't have been surprised. I walked to the front door and began fiddling with one of the thousand locks that ran along the side, but after a few quick beeps the locks simultaneously receded and the door pushed open.

Ax froze, blinked, his emerald eyes flashing with *something* as he stared back at me. And in return, my eyes popped, staring back. The six-foot-three mountain man stood before me in a dark navy suit, complete with black wing tips and a pink tie.

Pink.

Because real men wore pink. Or perhaps because he welcomed anyone who challenged it.

His disheveled hair had been scrubbed clean, the ends still wet from a shower. His beard, trimmed to five-o'clock shadow perfection. Clean, poised, mind-numbingly sexy. If he were uncomfortable, he didn't show it. Badass former Marine Axel Steele was as comfortable in his designer Gucci suit as he was in army fatigues and ATAC boots.

He scanned me from head to toe, slowly, unapologetically, every inch heating under the simmer of his gaze.

The instant racing of my heart threw me off. I tore my eyes away and took a step back.

"Would you like to come in?" I blinked. What the hell was that? Inviting him into his own cabin? "Sorry, I mean, come on in."

The corner of his lip twitched. Dammit, he knew he threw me off.

I shut the door as he took off through the living room without a word, scanning the doors and windows, meticulously checking every nook and cranny. His laser focus stopped on the wine glass sitting on the kitchen counter, then shifted to me.

I smiled and innocently shrugged. "It's after five." I'd be damned if he judged me for a glass of wine, or three.

"Is it okay?"

"What?"

"The wine."

"Oh. Yes. Thank you."

He returned his attention back to his examination of the walls. "Leave a list for Celeste with whatever you need, she'll get it."

I frowned. Did he think because it wasn't a hundred-dollar bottle of wine that I wouldn't think it was acceptable to me? Did he really think I was that big of a spoiled brat? Then I cursed myself and the insecurities that I tried so hard to push away.

He checked the deck, then stepped back inside and scanned the doorframe, squatting to his knees. This guy was thorough... and I really didn't mind watching him squat.

"Who's the artist?" I asked.

"What?" He asked, keeping his focus on the lock.

"The paintings on the walls."

"A local artist."

"They're beautiful."

He glanced up at me for a moment, then stood and

stepped past me. He disappeared into the bedroom. I followed. After checking the windows he stepped into the bathroom and stopped cold, locking on a pair of lace panties dangling out the side of my suitcase.

I grinned at his reaction. The guy could dismantle an IED while under heavy gunfire but a pair of panties? Stopped him dead in his tracks.

"They're panties. Women wear them under clothes."

"Panties, I'm familiar with. A single suitcase, I am not."

I laughed, he shot me a wink, then stepped around the case and checked the window behind the clawfoot soaking tub... I decided I wanted both—him and a bubble bath—right that minute.

He checked the closet. "Really? Only one case?"

"The rest are in my Maybach, with my diamonds. Twelve suitcases, Louis Vuitton. Vintage."

"Chevies'll get you past the pavement, Samsonite will get you past the chip on your shoulder."

"I was joking." I narrowed my eyes. "And what chip on my shoulder?"

"The green one."

Money.

He stepped passed me with a *'Scuse me*, then sauntered into the living room.

My brows shot up. I followed him. "Is there some sort of problem you have with me that I'm unaware of? Mr. *Steele.*" Okay, so the wine had kicked in.

"It's Ax."

"Axel."

"Just Ax."

"*Ax.*"

He checked his watch. "We need to get on."

"Wait." I plucked my wine glass from the counter. "Answer my question."

A breath escaped his lips, a subtle annoyance. "There won't be a problem as long as you do as I say, and don't do as I say, for that matter."

Eyeing him over the rim of my glass, I chugged the rest of my wine. Because I could. And it was after five.

He watched, unimpressed at this childish display.

I set the glass down and almost vomited.

Touché, universe, touché.

"Would you like me to bring the bottle?"

"Because I'm an alcoholic like all rich people?"

He nodded to my shoulder. The chip. The green one.

Got it. Message received. And not entirely inaccurate, I might add.

He checked his watch again, making me feel like *I* was causing us to be late. Reminding me that *he* was in charge.

"Before we leave, a talk. As I was saying, we won't have a problem as long as you do as I say—"

"And don't do..."

"Right. Tonight, at this party, you stick with me, close to me, and Erika, never, ever leave my side. Do you understand?"

"Yes, *sir.*"

He stared at me.

I rolled my eyes.

"*Yes,* I understand."

"Do you? Because you need to be clear that you signed on the dotted line for our services, Miss Zajac. And at the risk of being wrong, I'm guessing you're not one who usually follows orders. From anyone."

I swallowed deeply, feeling like particles of my dress

were falling off with each of his words. I didn't like how he was reading me. So precisely.

He continued, "While you're here, at Steele Shadows Security, you will follow orders. My orders. Or two things will happen, either we release you as our client, or you can leave on your own accord. Understood?"

"On second thought, Ax, grab that bottle of wine."

12

AXEL

 *R*ed wine in hand and attitude to match, Erika gripped my hand, *allowing me,* to help her into the passenger side of my truck. My eyes lingered on the pale, smooth skin of her bare back framed by the backless dress.

What a fucking dress. The front was a siren's deception of elegant, all-class, leaving only her long, slender neck and face exposed. Then, the back, *goddamn* that back, a vision worthy of whiplash and loss of focus on anything other than the curve of her spine, like the gold at the end of the rainbow. The velvet, soft like the comforter I'd like to throw her onto. The cut of the back like an arrow, guiding me to her deliciously round ass.

As if I needed help locating those curves.

All that alone was worthy of bringing any man to his knees, but it wasn't until I saw the hint of a tattoo down her side that I lost all perception of time and space—other than the lack of it in my pants all of a sudden.

Freckles, curves, tattoos.

Shit.

I'd about lost it watching Wolf toss her around the mat, their skin to skin contact igniting a protective streak inside me like a flash of lightning. It threw me off. Big time. We'd done the same dog and pony show with dozens of female clients, and never, not once, did I react with such hostility. Such *possessiveness.*

The girl was throwing me off. And being thrown off was not normal for this Steele brother.

I slid behind the wheel, clicked the high beams and made my way down the driveway.

"Who's that?" Erika glanced back at the black truck pulling out of a side road.

"My brother."

"The twin?"

"No, Gunner."

"What's he doing?"

"Joining us."

She glanced back again, and I caught a scent of her perfume. Not floral, feminine, but something smooth and citrusy. Something that reminded me of white sands and sapphire blue beaches.

Something that made me envision her in a bikini... then that bikini on my bedroom floor. I'd worn a lot of suits in my day, hated every second of it, but I wore them well. But this woman had me feeling a little hot around the neck. I cracked the window, and shifted my pubescent focus to where it should be—on making sure this damn party went as smoothly as possible.

"Once we get there, you'll make your rounds, try to get your eyes on as many people as possible, then we hit the road. Thirty minutes, tops."

"Thirty minutes? You can't be serious."

"Listen, tonight is not about socializing and kissing ass.

You're only going to see if you recognize anyone. In my mind that shouldn't even take thirty minutes."

"Have you ever been to a masquerade ball before?"

"Masquerade?"

"Yeah." She reached into her fancy handbag and pulled out a black mask with, God help me, black lace and gold feathers. She slipped it on.

A knot formed in my throat the size of a baseball, almost as big as what was forming in my pants.

"People wear masks to Masquerade balls."

"Why is this the first time I'm hearing of this little detail?"

"Because I knew you'd nix the idea the moment I told you."

"Why, because even assuming he's there, there's no way in hell you'd be able to identify your kidnapper considering half his face is going to be covered anyway."

She removed the mask, to my dismay. "It's the exact reason that I think he'd be more likely to show. He'll get to hunt behind a mask."

My grip tightened around the steering wheel. "I need you to be one-hundred percent up front with me going forward, you got it?"

She looked out the window confirming every bit of my suspicion that this woman wasn't telling me something.

"You got that, Erika? Up front. With everything."

"Got it."

"Alright, now, tell me about your half brother."

She frowned. "What about him?"

"I'm no head doctor but it doesn't appear you two have the best relationship."

She snorted, then took a second to gather her thoughts. Definitely more to this story.

"We have the same dad, different moms. They had me when Filip was twelve, and honestly, I don't think he cared for me from day one. After my mom left, things got worse, you could say. I think in Filip's mind, I was this little orphan that he was forced to live with. Dad started grooming Filip to take over the family business the moment he turned sixteen—"

"And you?"

She laughed. "No, I had no interest in finance. Trust me."

I waited, wanting to hear what her interests were. No dice.

She continued, "Then, I moved out at sixteen, dad died shortly after, and Filip took over with bells on. Worked side by side with Reid, and I will say, he stepped up to the plate."

"Kinda breezed over some stuff there."

She shrugged, again, avoiding eye contact. "I was a bit rebellious, I guess."

"Where did you move to?"

"Family."

Her single word response was as loaded as a machine gun. She continued, "Anyway, after I left, Filip and I pretty much quit talking. No big deal. He took over dad's business and doubled the company's size and all was right in the world."

"And you didn't take a position within the company?"

"Nope."

"Went to a few parties." She grinned.

"Well that's it then."

"What's it?"

"You stole the show. That's why your brother doesn't like you."

"Ha. Funny. I didn't steal the show."

"If you wore a dress like that you did."

She smiled.

I continued, "I bet if you had been *paying attention*, you'd notice all sorts of attention from men."

"After Wolf's little lesson today, I'll always *pay attention*." She shook her head, then said, "I'm a single, young woman from a family who fell into some money... that alone gets me all sorts of looks from bored, married men."

I looked at her in the passenger seat, the once soft lines of her face now hard. "There's a lot of single, young, rich girls, and trust me, not all get looks from men."

"Fine. It's the bunions."

My eyebrows popped up. "Bunions, huh?"

"Oh yeah, brutal. Like walnuts on the sides of my big toes."

I grinned, catching a soft grin on her lips, too. Although this woman had every reason in the book to be cocky, she was self-deprecating, and if anything, fighting some sort of deep-rooted insecurity. An insecurity that would take much more than a bottle of wine to reveal.

"Well, despite the bowling balls on your feet, your brother wouldn't have convinced you to come to us if he didn't care about you, right?"

"First, Detective Jagger convinced me. And, *no*. My brother cares about the business. He's afraid the guy is going to kidnap me and he'll get another ransom call. It's not about me, it's about money—Filip's favorite thing."

"How long has Harrison been a part of the company?"

"Day one."

We crossed a one-lane covered bridge, the water rushing beneath it from a recent rain. The road took a turn, snaking through a narrow valley that cut through two soaring mountains.

"You know where you're going?"

I cut her a glance.

"Sorry. Of course you do." She chuckled. "Seriously, though, the gala's being held at a famous hotel all the way out here? That doesn't—"

Before she could finish, the truck bumped around a hair-pin corner that faded into twinkling lampposts. The long, steep paved road was lined with every expensive car known to man, the silver glow of the moon sparkling off the newly painted exteriors.

We passed a wooden sign that read *Welcome to the Half Moon Hotel.* Clipped to the bottom, *Closed, Private Event.* And below that, a trio of Jack-o-lanterns, complete with glowing round eyes and fangs.

"What is this place?"

"Haunting."

Wide-eyed, she glanced at me as we ascended the steep mountain. Surrounded by miles and miles of woods, the massive, old hotel came into view, twinkling through the darkness. The front of the hotel had a covered circle drive underneath columns that stretched up to a fourth-floor balcony bar, where stone gargoyles peered at the property below. Hay bales, scarecrows, and pumpkins decorated the front steps where the area's wealthiest mingled in shimmering dresses and long-stemmed champagne glasses, and fancy masks covering their faces. Candles flickered in the windows.

Haunting—and fitting for the evening's events.

We drove past the circle drive where a shiny 1959 Cadillac Eldorado was parked.

"Where are you going?"

I braked down a steep hill, and after a quick glance at

the rearview mirror, turned into a lot marked *Employee Parking*.

Erika glanced over her shoulder. "Where's Gunner?"

"Around. Stay."

Her neck whipped toward me, followed by muffled obscenities as I shut the door behind me. I smirked as I walked around the hood.

She flung open the passenger door. "I'm *not* a dog."

"Tell that to your feet."

She laughed.

My heart kicked.

"You ready?"

I helped her out of the truck and she looped her arm around mine, inciting a surprising feeling of pride. One that I realized I hadn't felt in a while. Or, maybe ever. Erika wasn't only beautiful, it was the way she carried herself. There was an understated elegance to her that somehow went hand in hand with the intricate tattoos coloring her skin. She was something else.

We started up the hill. "Remember, you do *not* leave my side. Understood?"

"Yes," an exasperated sigh. "My *God,* yes, *Ax."*

"Just making sure. You get that we're not undercover or anything. That this isn't some *super-cool* undercover sting op in a low-budget spy flick. You're you, I'm your date, and we are attending this thing for the sole purpose to see if anything stands out to you, if anything rings a bell that might lead to a break in this case. That's it."

"Do you know that you can be kind of condescending?"

I stopped cold and turned to her. "Erika, I don't mess around when it comes to my job. You came to us for protection, and I'm calling the shots here. You're free to walk whenever, but until that day, I call the shots. And I take this job—protecting you—very seriously."

She blinked up at me. "You really should think about taking a vacation. A long vacation."

"*Christ,*" I muttered, then yanked my arm around her and pulled her into step with me. "Let's go."

"I'm not as big of an idiot as you think I am, Ax. I'm not going to go in there and interview everyone I meet. But I'm also not going to let this thing go. I know I can help, and I will."

I noticed the spark of fight in her eyes that I'd seen a few times already. And I couldn't help but wonder... why?

Why wouldn't she leave this to the authorities? Why was she so hellbent on finding this guy herself?

Erika Zajac had secrets.

And I needed to figure out what those secrets were.

13

ERIKA

*I*t was a concerted effort not to grip Ax's arm as we stepped into the hotel. I felt like I'd taken ten shots of espresso, followed by three tequilas. Damn anxiety. I knew there'd be apprehension knowing that I could come face to face with the evil of my past, and present. But what I hadn't expected was feeling *fear.* That raw, ripe, pungent blanket threatening to cripple every step. And let me tell you, that creepy-ass hotel did nothing to help matters.

I scanned the masks, some turning in my direction as Ax scribbled our names on the sign-in sheet and we crossed the expansive lobby.

What would I do if I saw him?

Ax's concern that I'd go nuts wasn't too far from the truth, but something told me that even if that was the case, if I did blow this *'super-cool undercover sting op'* that I was in good company. Hell, I'd be safe in the zombie apocalypse with Ax at my side.

So, I took a deep breath and forced my shoulders to relax, my hand to dangle from Ax's beefed up forearm, mirroring the women being escorted by their husbands... or their dads. Your guess was as good as mine on that one.

One thing was for sure, every hoity toity charity gala was the same, with the same stuffy people with their shiny cars and canned laughter. The only thing different with this party was the location. It was as if I'd stepped into a 1950's horror movie. The hotel had obviously been renovated, but the owners had opted to keep the same dark, dated feel to the place, with antique furniture and fixtures throughout. This haunting ambiance was compounded by the amount of long stemmed candles that cast dark shadows across the walls resembling ghosts swaying back and forth. Mirroring the circle drive, more wickedly-grinning Jack-o-lanterns, ornate pumpkins, and fall foliage decorated the lobby.

Creepy, creepy, and creepy.

"Oh, dear Axel, what a pleasure to see you." A heavily botoxed woman—impossible to tell her age—stepped over and extended her dainty, frail arm. A long string of pearls wrapped her wrists, matching the ones on her fingers. "I'm so sorry to hear about your brother, and of course your father."

My gaze lifted to Ax, aware of his father's passing but unaware of his brother's.

"Thank you, Mrs. Bluestein." A response as stoic as his stance. "This is Erika Zajac."

"My, look at that tattoo." Her eyes flickered to the rose on my wrist and she pulled her hand away. My lip tugged in amusement. They were all the same. Pity a young woman who'd marked herself up as if I must've been under some sort of new psychedelic drug, or held at gunpoint. I knew Mrs. Bluestein, a narrow-minded housewife whose idea of a good time was following her staff around her multi-million dollar mansion pointing out things they could "improve on."

"Zajac... What an *interesting* last name you have..."

"It's Polish."

"Oh. Polish." She gave me the once-over. Her brow tipped up. "And what do you do, Miss Zajac?"

"She's my full-time girlfriend. Excuse us, Mrs. Bluestein."

I'd opened my mouth to answer her question with one of the dozen profanity-laced responses I had on the tip of my tongue, but reading me like a clock, Ax pulled me away.

"Hey, we were just getting started there." I said with a grin.

He grinned back. "Yeah, I had no doubt you were. Want to tell me what you had loaded up there, hot rod?"

"Well, I was going to go with transsexual bi-racial pearl thief, then, maybe full-time recovering anti-Semite, but no, for Mrs. Bluestein, I'd be a socialist Rabbi turned vodka brewer—one Polack of three that it took to screw in a lightbulb. I think that one covered all the bases."

His grin widened to an all-out smile, with a hint of pride. I liked it. I liked that I made him smile. I also realized that he had no idea what I did for my *job*. Which, didn't surprise me, because no one did.

"And... thank you." I said.

"You're welcome. She's old money, old mindset."

"No, I meant for making me your girlfriend for the evening." I winked. "Just joking. Yes, thanks for pulling me away. Although, seriously, I get the feeling that being your girlfriend is always a temporary position, anyway."

"Interns are hot, aren't they?" He winked back.

A moment passed. "I read about your father, and I'm sorry. But, your brother? What's—"

"It's being handled."

My brows knit together. 'It's being handled.' It was such

an odd response that I let it go. He obviously didn't want to talk about it, and I didn't want to press.

We didn't make it ten more steps before being waylaid again. Apparently, Axel Steele was well known within the community. I scanned the crowd of masks, looking for our purpose of the evening. The silence of the cellar, the smell, the memories materializing in my head like a clouded nightmare.

He had to be there. I knew it.

I turned back to Ax, who'd been pulled into another circle of gossips. This one though, a group of men and one woman, all masked except for one. I watched the man's focus on Ax, the kind that was a thinly veiled attempt to make you think you were the only person in the room. The posturing, the shiny Rolex, the smooth flow of his laugh.

A politician, by all counts.

And not to my surprise, Ax held his own. And then some.

"Erika," Ax turned to me as I stepped up. "This is Senator Inglewood and his wife, Marianne, and Senator Inglewood's Chief of Staff, Antonio Perez." He turned back. "This is Erika Zajac."

My brows tipped up as my stomach dropped. I didn't know how exactly, but I knew that Inglewood was being "looked at" in a loose connection with the incident.

A tingle moved up my spine like goblin's fingers. The world seemed to stand still around us as we shook hands, inciting a blow to my pulse that sent it racing in my chest. But it was the faceless gaze from his Chief of Staff that kept pulling my attention. A wolf mask, black, cut off below his nose. Smooth, tanned skin and thin, curved lips pointed directly at me. While Inglewood appeared to be in his sixties, the masked man appeared much younger, perhaps mid-forties. The whites of his eyes shifted to Ax before settling back on me.

"Nice to meet you, Miss Zajac." Senator Inglewood pulled my focus back to him. He dropped his hand, a scabbed scratch at the top of his thumb catching my attention.

Ax's hand slid onto my lower back.

The perfection of Inglewood's wife, all flawless skin and impeccable manners, lightly shook my hand.

"Pleasure to meet you, Miss Zajac."

"You as well."

"So, tell me, what—"

Senator Inglewood interrupted and motioned to the sweeping windows. "The party is out on the back terrace. Shall we?"

Marianne looped her arm around mine and guided me across the lobby, with Ax, Senator Inglewood, and Antonio Perez close behind.

"Such lovely weather we're having, isn't it?" She said, "Rain is coming over the next few weeks. My chrysanthemums could sure use it..."

As Marianne drummed on about her garden, we stepped onto the expansive, stone terrace that overlooked rolling hills that faded into the woods.

"Senator, Marianne..."

"Excuse me, dear."

I nodded as Marianne pulled away, along with her husband and Perez, and joined another ass-kissing group.

The party was in full swing and Inglewood's campaign had spared no expense.

Bright stars twinkled above dozens of strings of lights that weaved throughout the oak trees that enclosed the terrace. Round tables with white tablecloths and dancing candles speckled the area. A band played smooth jazz in the corner, next to a full bar. The waitstaff served plates of seasonal delicacies and flutes of champagne. The men boasted in their pricey suits, the women glittering in their designer dresses.

"A regular Tuesday night at your place growing up?" Ax said in my ear.

I rolled my eyes with a grin. "No, my dad would've had more people."

"Of course."

"Did you notice the cut on Inglewood's hand?"

He guided me to the corner, stopping next to the thick stone railing that lined the terrace.

"I did."

"Could be from Jessa, or me, even."

Ax angled himself between me and the crowd, forcing my body into the corner. He had a full view of the party, and me, squarely secured behind him. Every one of Ax's moves were calculated, every turn of his head, every movement was centered around my protection. And he did it with such ease, such grace, it was almost undetectable.

"What do you know about his Chief of Staff?" I asked.

"Other than his immediate interest in you?"

"Exactly."

"I'm sure the feds are pulling everything they can about him, down to his underwear size."

"He gave me the creeps."

"He took interest in a beautiful woman." He said it in a matter-of-fact tone that had me wondering if I was ridiculous for taking it as a compliment. "Anything standing out to you?"

I shifted to the crowd. "No. Not yet." The tuxedos made it impossible to check for the black *V* tattoo I'd seen on my captor's forearm. The masks made it impossible to recognize even a profile, not that I'd seen much, anyway.

"Champagne?" A bleached-blonde waitress in a slinky back dress that barely covered her backside breezed up to Ax. I was invisible. I noticed the twinkle in her eye as she studied him, the subtle lick of her lips. The woman would have served herself on that platter if she could have, that much was obvious. What wasn't obvious was if Ax would let her... or if he had already.

He handed me a glass, then took one for himself.

"Thank you," he said.

The waitress winked and walked away, not even giving me a courtesy glance.

"Cheers." He said and we tapped glasses.

I watched him over the rim as I sipped. I didn't blame the waitress. Axel Steele was an unstoppable force of both worlds as he stood there in his designer suit, a five-o'clock shadow and brown hair mussed enough to let everyone know he didn't give a shit. An impossible mixture of dapper and rugged—and panty-dropping sexy. If the blonde would have known about the gun hidden on his hip, she might have dropped to her knees right then.

I realized then, that I didn't even know if Ax had a girlfriend. Or many, for that matter. Of course he did. There was no way a man that looked like that, with that kind of money, who specialized in saving damsels in distress didn't have women in his bed. Or many, for that matter.

It was just as well anyway.

Because I had my own secrets.

He glanced at his watch. "We've got exactly seventeen minutes left here."

"Are you that miserable?"

"I'm that punctual."

"Neurotic."

"Methodical."

"Tight-ass."

"Only on Saturday nights." He sipped.

My brow cocked. "I'm saying, you could stand to loosen up a bit. Can't you even try to enjoy yourself while we're here?"

He continued to scan the terrace.

"Of course not." I shook my head and gazed out at the crowd. "Look, over there, at that guy. Gold mask with stupid horns, knock-off suit, pony-tail, whiskey on the rocks while everyone else is drinking champagne, and a dip in his mouth the size of a walnut. Now *that* guy knows how to relax."

Gold-horned man turned toward me, a smile curving his lips.

"Looks like he'd like to relax with you."

"I don't do whiskey."

"Tequila."

"What?"

"It's a tequila. Not whiskey."

"How do you know that?"

"The color."

I squinted. "It's brown."

"Babe Ruth over there is drinking an Extra Anejo tequila, which is aged for over three years giving it a dark caramel color, and is one of the most expensive drinks here."

"You're a walking encyclopedia."

His lip twitched and he continued, "And, it's not a knock-off suit. By the slight puckering on his back shoulders, I'd say he's wearing a vintage, handmade Italian-made suit only available through special order. He's new money, and wants to fit in, and goes above and beyond to show it. But the tobacco in his mouth tells me he's yet to curb his southern roots where he grew up in a single-wide in the sticks."

"How do you know all this stuff?"

"It's simple, Erika. I pay attention."

"You should put that attention on Jeopardy."

"I'd rather use it to save someone's life." He cut me a side-eye.

"Oh, touché, Mr. Steele."

The corner of his lip curled.

I leaned against the railing, scanning the crowd for the hundredth time. "Nothing..." I muttered.

"Stop looking at people."

"What? That's the entire reason we're here unless I'm missing something..."

"No, I don't mean it like that, I mean tune into your instinct when you look at them."

I thought of the feeling when Senator Inglewood shook my hand.

He continued, "Human beings have built-in security systems. The problem is, most people don't use them. Instead, we're consumed with whatever craving, desire, sin, is our primary focus of that moment. We push aside all common sense. I see it all the time with victims."

"Sometimes it's good to *give in* every once in a while, Ax. Stay up late, have that extra drink, call in sick to work and watch football all day."

He shook his head. "That's exactly what I'm talking about. Everyone listens to their egos, is driven by it, and tunes out our most basic survival instinct. Combining that with living in a society where we rely on fallible things like technology to do everything for us, hell, it's a miracle most of us make it across the street." He glanced at me, then back to that crowd. "That day you went hiking on Red Rock Trail. The day you found the trap door. Your instincts were telling you not to go to it, not to open it, am I right?"

I glanced down, remembering the nerves shooting through my system as I'd spotted the door beyond the boulder. I remember the nerves before I even stepped into the clearing.

"Maybe it wasn't a voice in your head audibly to go back, but you felt it in your body. Your stomach probably. Am I right?"

I nodded.

"Would you like to know why, Erika?"

I sipped. "I have a feeling you're going to tell me, no matter what."

The slightest grin, then, "The human body is broken up into two systems, the sympathetic and parasympathetic. The sympathetic is your flight-or-fight branch. So, when you have an immediate reaction to something, whether you feel scared, nervous, apprehensive, excited, attracted, or whatever, the sympathetic system releases adrenaline, which kicks up your heart rate and glucose levels, and pulls blood away from your gut. This reduction of blood flow is that butterfly sensation you feel. In some cases, in instances of attraction or excitement, dopamine is released giving the same sensation. But on *that* day, it was fear and nervousness that sent your stomach swirling." He sipped as he slid into his comfort zone—his *real* comfort zone—an intellectual conversation. Providing facts to back up a claim. He continued.

"That feeling you felt right before you opened the trap door? That, *that,* Erika, was your survival instinct kicking in. Your body's sixth sense screaming at you. But did you stop? Did you go back?" He stared at me for a moment. "No.

Because your ego—the most powerful and destructive part of the human body—was telling you to indulge your curiosities. You allowed your ignorant ego to get the best of you. Your ego was stronger than you were."

It was like a punch in the gut. I wanted to argue, call him a dick, but the truth was he was right.

"Pay attention Erika." His gaze leveled mine. "From this point forward, you need to pay more attention. To where you are, where you are going, who you see, and who you're with."

There was a caution in his tone, a warning that made me wonder what he wasn't telling me.

Our eyes locked, the intensity sending my stomach flip-flopping. Thanks to Bill Nye, I knew that it wasn't just a near-death experience that kicked up my sympathetic system, but also, a single man named Axel Steele. My reaction to the man standing next to me was as powerful as when my life was threatened. It was a mind-boggling, jarring thought.

And that moment I knew I was in trouble.

As if reading my thoughts, he set down his Champagne glass and grabbed my hand.

My pulse quickened from the dopamine flooding my system—apparently.

He pulled me away from the railing.

"Where are we going?" I asked.

"You said I needed to loosen up." He pulled me onto the dance floor.

"No. *No,* I don't dance, Ax." My eyes darted around the fancy couples swaying flawlessly to the beat of the jazz band. "And besides, you said the number one priority of personal security is to never take your eye off the ball—"

I was whipped around with a force that had my head

spinning. His hand caught mine, lifted, then pulled my body to his. Our bodies collided, the breath escaping my lips with a grunt. He looked down at me, inches from my face. My heart skipped a beat as I stared back at him, powerless against his grip, powerless against those eyes, powerless against the way he made me feel in his arms.

"I said to never lose focus." His hips pressed against mine. "And tonight, you're mine."

His grip tightened as he spun me around and we fell into a rhythm that matched the music. He led me with the ease and confidence of someone who'd spent their entire life guiding women across a dance floor. The guy knew how to dance. *Really* dance. It was yet another surprise from the rugged woodsman who'd spent most his life hunting America's most wanted.

He led, I followed, allowing him to spin me across the floor as if we'd done it a million times before. We stared into each other's eyes, the heat of his touch running like sunbeams under his fingertips.

My daze drifted to his lips. Maybe it was the champagne, or the dozens of twinkling lights reflecting in those stormy eyes, but at that moment, all I wanted to do was kiss him. For *him* to kiss *me.*

My eyes met his and there was no mistaking he'd read my thoughts.

Butterflies, as he leaned down.

My lids drifted closed.

And then it happened—

Crack!

Bodies hit the floor around us with shrill screams and chaotic shouts. My breath knocked out of my lungs as my body hit the terrace floor as another *crack* vibrated through the air. Ax's body covered mine as everything drifted in and out of slow motion. The shattering stone pillar inches from my head, more gunshots echoing through the woods. The screams, oh God, the screams.

And the warm pool of blood saturating the ground beneath me.

14

ERIKA

"*A*re you hurt?"

I blinked, focusing on Ax, his words fading in and out like some daydream being realized. A nightmare. I blinked again, wondering if I had some sort of concussion creating the fog in my head.

He cupped my face, and I noticed the screams had stopped. There was shuffling, moaning, sobbing, but the screams had dissipated along with the gunshots. A stillness settled around us, an eerie quietness I'll never, ever forget.

"Erika, I need you to answer me. Are you hurt?"

My fingertips moved in the warm blood oozing over the stone floor beneath me. Ax checked me over, resigning to the fact that I couldn't push out a word.

Someone had shot at us, at me.

And then, like an unstoppable force, it started, the wave of heat over my body, instant sweat soaking my skin. Constricting lungs over a palpitating heart. A wave of tingles telling me it was coming. My heart skipped wildly in my chest, the sudden feeling of being suffocated, the oxygen around me too shallow to fill my gasping breaths. Then, the panic, the claustrophobia from being pinned to the ground. The blood, a poison about to dissolve my skin in a slow, agonizing death.

"Get off me," I squeaked out, the panic overwhelming me. "Get *off* me," I screamed, swatting, kicking Ax in a mad hysteria. Instead of rolling off me, he pinned my arms on either side of my head, his gaze pinning me with more force than the grip around my wrists.

"Breathe." He demanded.

I squirmed against him, bucking like an animal.

"*Stop*. Look at me, baby. *Erika*. Look at me."

I found his words like a light through the darkness. Sweat rolled down my face as I tried to tell my brain to focus on him.

"Look at *me*." I felt his hands sweeping over my body, still scanning for gunshot wounds.

I squinted at the blurriness, my focus darting around the string of lights above us.

"Look at me."

My eyes finally met his.

"Good. Breathe. Now, breathe, Erika."

I inhaled shakily, tears threatening.

"Exhale... Good girl, another, watch me."

We breathed together, eyes locked together, me, in some sort of half-conscious state letting him lead me through the haze. I felt him, the power of his calmness, the comfort of his voice, the strength in knowing that I was completely, one-hundred percent safe underneath that man.

Together we breathed as one.

My pulse started to calm, the sweat over my skin beginning to cool.

The intensity in his face softened. "Good girl. Good girl. Keep breathing."

I heard the sound of Gunner's voice, a faint sound from a tin box.

Ax pressed his finger to an ear piece I hadn't even realized he was wearing. "Ten four, twenty seconds." He shifted his attention back to me. "Okay, I need to get you out of here, okay?"

Inhaling, I nodded.

"Good." He looked from left to right then focused again on me. "I want you to keep your eyes up and straight ahead, do you understand? Do *not* look around. Do not look down. Got it?"

"Yes."

"On three, we're going to get up and run like hell. You'll follow my lead, do you understand?"

"Yes," I nodded feverishly. "Yes."

"Okay." He smiled. "You've got this. Let's get you out of here."

My heart kicked up again.

"Erika. I need you to stay with me right now. On three. One..." He lifted off me. "Two..." his hands gripped my shoulders. *"Three."* My body was lifted from the ground like a rag doll. We lunged to the side, Ax's body shielding me as we darted across the terrace.

Bodies were everywhere. I locked on the expressionless eyes of a woman, blood snaking from her body to where mine had been.

I stumbled on my dress.

"Stay with me, Erika." Ax pulled me to him and all but threw me off the terrace and onto a narrow sidewalk that skirted the side of the hotel. Sirens wailed in the distance, and again, I noticed how eerily silent the air was around me. It was even as if the animals in the woods had stopped moving, the breeze had halted, leaving only the unmeasurable weight of tragedy hanging like a thick blanket in the air.

Ax moved beside me, pulling me as if he'd walked that route a thousand times. I surveyed the woods around us, an endless blackness where a psycho with a rifle had taken cover and destroyed the evening.

A small light pulled my attention to a truck in front of us that I hadn't even noticed. The door opened, and I was pushed inside, followed by Ax.

"She hit?" Gunner asked calmly as the tires spun rocks into the air.

"No."

My body was guided onto the floorboard, my head shoved into Ax's lap.

"Take the south pass." Ax said, matching the calm tone of his brother.

Gunner gassed it and after a loud *pop*, followed by the sound of a chain dragging along the side of the truck, we descended into the woods. Sirens screamed through the air behind us.

I gripped onto Ax's legs, my body shifting with each bump, my mind racing to put together the pieces of what had just happened.

"Did you see him?" Ax asked his brother while his hand found the top of my head, and began to stroke.

"No. He was southwest, somewhere in the woods. Probably a bluff or cliff. Based on the echo, I'm guessing a good hundred yards out."

"Agreed. A night scope—"

"Definitely. How many bodies?"

"Two. One in the stomach, the other a torso shot."

My stomach dropped to my feet. I caught Gunner glancing down at me.

Two bodies.

Two *more* bodies.

A minute later, we rolled to a stop.

"See you at the house."

"Thanks, brother."

Ax opened the door and gripped my hand. As he guided me out of the truck, my gaze was fixed on the direction we'd just come from.

Two more bodies.

My blood began to boil, plans spinning in my head—too many, and none sticking. I looked around in an attempt to get my bearings. We were out in the middle of the woods surrounded by soaring pines and thick underbrush that faded into the dark night. No road... no voices, sirens, screams. Only Ax's black truck, almost invisible behind the bushes.

"How did you... when did you move your truck?"

"I didn't." He scanned the woods as he addressed me. "Gunner did. Get in."

After shutting my door, he slid behind the wheel. The truck came to life with a low growl and with only the running lights as a guide, we took off through the woods. Twigs and branches swiped the side of his brand-new truck. He didn't even flinch. Other than the locked jaw and occasional glance in the rearview mirror, he was somewhere else, his mind running as quickly as my own.

"Who were they? The two?"

A moment passed as he seemed to be deciding something. "A man, who was dancing with the woman to our left. And the woman, Doris White, who was dancing with her husband of forty-three years, to our right."

"The two people that were shot were directly on either side of us?"

"Yes."

"*Ax.*" I turned to him. "*I* was the target. You understand that, right?"

The twitch of his jaw was enough of an answer for me.

"Then you'll understand why I have to do what I have to do." I put my hand on the handle. "Stop. Stop the truck. I have to go back. I'm *going back*—"

"Don't even think about it," the seething warning was punctuated with the clicking of the lock.

"Ax—"

"My job is to protect you. Everything else comes second."

"*Ax*—"

"How do we know the guy isn't still in the woods waiting for you to show your face on the terrace again, or in a window of the hotel?" He paused. "And we don't know for complete certain that you were the target."

"*Bullshit.* Don't patronize me."

"Listen, the cops are there and I'm sure they'll call in all available resources. They'll find him."

With a snort, I looked out the window, disgust, disdain, and disrespect for the men in blue churning deep in my stomach. Ax had no idea how much the cops, and 'all available resources' had let me down in the past. He had no freaking clue.

And it was going to end.

Tonight.

With a deep bump, we emerged from the woods onto a narrow dirt road. Thick clouds had drifted over the moon, blackening the night as dark as ink. He flicked on his lights.

"Where are we?"

"Close to the cabin."

He veered off the road, hung another left, then a quick

right, and the woods opened up to a small clearing where nestled in the back sat Cabin 2, alit with a golden porch light and dim lights inside. He stopped, shoved the truck into park.

"I'm going back." I informed him.

"You're out of your mind." He pushed out of the truck and slammed the door with a force that had a tingle shooting up my spine.

I shoved out my door.

"Get in the cabin." He was by my side in an instant, but not because he wanted to, it was because he was shielding me from the woods behind us. I side-stepped away, irritated, pissed, emotional, whatever.

"I'm going back to that hotel, Ax. There are three deaths associated with what happened now. Something *I* am involved in. Jessa, and now the two poor people who were dancing next to us." I spun around almost as fast as my mind was. "Where's my car?"

He grabbed my arm.

"Get off me," I snapped. "Where's my car—"

Before I could finish the words, I was lifted into the air and thrown over his shoulder, my head bouncing off his lower back, my dress coming up over my thighs.

"Ouch! That *hurt."*

"Too bad."

"Put me *down."* I struggled against him like a raccoon caught in a bear trap—useless. Exactly as he intended. "Where's my car?"

"Your Tahoe is in our garage and your keys are in our safe."

"Take me. Now. I want them."

"No." He stomped up the cabin steps.

After a few beeps, the door pushed open. My feet hit the floor with a thud, pissing me off even more.

"*Listen, Ax,* I'm not going to be held here against my will. It's my decision. Not yours, not my brother's, not anyone's but *mine.*" I narrowed my eyes and closed the inches between us. "If you won't get me my car, I'll *walk* back to the hotel." I pushed past him, through the door.

"*Erika.*"

His voice boomed against the silence, the thunderous tone sending the hair on the back of my neck standing up. My instinct was to stop, but I forced myself to keep walking. What the hell was I doing? I had no clue. He and I both knew I wasn't going to walk back to that hotel. Especially in an evening gown and six inch heels. All I knew was that I felt trapped, chained down, and true to form, I wanted to *run.*

Run, run, run, as I always did.

I didn't see him, I didn't hear him, but suddenly, I knew without question he was right behind me.

"Go. Leave me alone." I stomped into the woods resembling a toddler having a fit. "*Go.*"

"You want to walk across the mountains in the middle of the night, go for it. But you need to understand you're on your own. I'm out."

I stopped.

"I'm. Out." He repeated, cold as ice.

I spun around. Ax was nothing but a dark silhouette in front of me, a menacing outline against the cabin lights. The whites of his eyes barely visible, the hostility on full display.

"You're *out?*"

"That's right. I'm done. Your keys will be in the ignition when you make it back."

I blinked. "Okay, then. That's it. And that's fine with me."

I'd made it all my freaking life without a man's help, and I sure as hell could do it again. I turned and walked away, pushing through a thicket of bushes.

A solid minute passed.

Finally—

"God *dammit!* Erika, *stop."*

His shout echoed through the woods, and this time, I stopped on a dime.

"Turn around."

I did.

And he was there, again, two inches in front of me. And he was *pissed.*

"I am not in the fucking mood for this, and I'm not going to deal with your childish antics, Erika. You *will* go back into the cabin, or I will haul you back there myself."

I started to say something but was cut off.

"No. Walk."

"Why? Why won't you let me go?"

The hard lines of his jaw reflected in the moonlight as he stared down at me.

"Because, Erika, you're being hunted."

And that was exactly the point.

15

ERIKA

*a*x set out across the room, methodically checking the windows, locks—for the second time that evening—as he told me all about the Black V's in an attempt to convince me of what kind of trouble I was really in.

Little did he know, I knew all of it.

And little did he know that revenge was much more powerful than money and power.

Thunder rumbled in the distance.

"Why didn't you tell me all this? From the beginning?" I asked as I kicked off my heels.

"You didn't need to know. I needed to get a better understanding of what we were up against before you learned the whole story. Now you know it and I need you to get your head out of your ass, and understand that the threat is real. Understand that the decisions of day to day fall under me, and they are always in your best interest. I've done this my entire life. I need you to understand that."

I nodded, fully understanding what it meant to groom your entire life for something.

"Now, Erika..." His eyes narrowed. "Now, I need to know what *you're* keeping from *me.*"

A knot formed in my throat and I forced myself not to look away.

"I don't know what you're talking about." I lied.

"Don't patronize me."

≈

Axel

I watched her shift her weight, the subtle twitch of her jaw. The effort she was making to keep eye contact. If nothing came from this, I sure as hell needed to give the woman a lesson in beating a lie detector. But something *was* going to come out of this conversation, because I wasn't going to leave until Erika Zajac told me what she was holding back from me.

Finally, she tipped her head back and blew out a breath, my eyes drifting down to her long, pale neck stretching against the exhale.

"What do you want to know?" She asked.

I walked to the liquor cabinet and pulled down a bottle of vodka.

"Everything." I sat it in front of her.

"Because vodka is the key to unlocking Polish secrets?"

"Stop deflecting."

Her face softened and after taking a shot—without a wince—she handed it to me. I did the same and almost spat it into the sink. Never understood the lure of a liquor that tasted like rubbing alcohol.

With that symbol of bonding out of the way, she began.

"You know that I moved out of my dad's house when I

was sixteen. Well, I moved in with my grandmother, my Dad's mom, who brought him to the states when he was a baby."

"Where's your mom?"

I snorted. "Villa in the south of France. Divorced my Dad after he hit it big, took half his money and left the country. Me included."

"That had to have made an impact."

I shrugged. "Not really. My grandma was my mom. Baba, I called her." Fondness sparked in her eyes. "I remember, even at such a young age, her telling me stories of Poland and of the first few times she visited America. She said it was the land of opportunity. It's funny, growing up here, to see people disrespect the American flag and all it stands for, when so many people dream of living in this country."

Unfortunately, I knew both sides of that pendulum. I knew the beauty and opportunity of the country—the American Dream was a real and obtainable thing. But every fantasy has a dark side, an evil, and as the director of the NSA, my father had seen his fair share of internal corruption and had lost his life because of it. Yes, I knew all about the American Dream, and about the secrets it would kill to protect.

She continued, "My grandma and my father had a falling out when he'd started making his money. He'd changed, I'd seen it first-hand. He turned into a greedy, conniving businessman. Baba never accepted a penny from him, and he never pushed, trust me on that. I respected her so much. So despite my sixteen years of a posh, spoiled brat lifestyle, when I moved in with Baba, I realized what it was like to be poor. The mother of a rich businessman—who would have never had the opportunities he did if she wouldn't have made the sacrifices for him—was living in a one bedroom apartment with no air conditioning or cable, and barely enough to eat. It was shocking, to say the least. But we'd made it, and we were happy. When I moved in, Baba was working at a local grocery store during the day and a waitress in the nights. A year later, she'd saved up enough money to open her own restaurant." A smile softened her face. She was proud of her grandmother, the only female figure in her life, apparently. "I was a cook and waitress at the restaurant every second that I wasn't in school. Baba always tried to get me to take time off, relax. She always told me to seize the moment. All we ever have is right now, she'd say. Live each day to the fullest. And I did. On my own terms. On her terms."

"And your brother?"

"We'd stopped talking. It was me and Baba, scraping to make ends meet, and dad and Filip shopping for yachts. And I didn't care. I loved it. I loved the feeling of working hard for something you got. There's a pride in it. I finally felt like I was worth something, ironically. I was happy." Her face dropped. "Until the day that changed our lives forever."

I wanted to push off the counter, hold her hand for the rest of what I knew was going to be a terrible story. But somehow I knew that wasn't what she wanted, needed.

She took another shot of vodka.

"We were closing up the restaurant one evening, April twenty-second to be exact. The building backed up to a long alley that led to a small stretch of woods. It was around midnight, and," she squinted, tilting her head to the ceiling, the memories taking her away. "It was a full moon, a million stars in the sky. I remember noticing how big it was, appreciating it, being thankful." She shook her head and looked down. "Then I remember my attention being pulled to three guys coming out of nowhere. I knew immediately that we were in danger."

"Your sixth sense."

"I guess so. I grabbed Baba's arm. There was something about the way they walked, a kind of amped up strut with their eyes glued to us. Looking back, I think they'd waited for us to come out. And then, they slid on black ski masks." She swallowed the knot in her throat. "I yanked at Baba, thinking we could make it to the street. But they were on us." Her voice cracked, her cheeks beginning to flush. "I'll never forget, Ax, I'll *never* forget. Baba turned to me with the sweetest, softest look in her eyes. Looking back, I think she knew. She knew what was about to happen. She pulled a ring from her finger that she always wore. She called it her bluebird ring. It had three tiny blue stones at the top. Anyway, she wrapped it in my palm. *Keep this, always,* she said. *It's a piece of me, your roots. I'm always with you.*" Erika's lip quivered, my stomach knotting. "Baba grabbed my face, cupping my cheeks in her hands, and said, *you've got a long, beautiful life ahead of you. I'll be right there with you. You make me so happy, my baby. I'm always with you.*" Tears streamed down her cheeks, dropping onto the gray velvet of her dress. "Then, she told me to run to the police station, a few blocks down. I remember her grip tightening around my face, the panic suddenly in her eyes. I started to cry at that point. She told me to run again, as they grabbed her, and I did. But not before I saw the arm of one of the guys, and the black *V* tattooed on it." Erika covered her mouth with her hand and stared out the window. She wasn't in the room with me anymore, she was there, back to that night. "I ran," she whispered. "Bawling my eyes out and gripping onto that ring. I was almost to the street when I realized I had a cell phone. I stopped dialed nine-one-one and, I don't know why, I ran back to the alley..."

She put her face in her hands and began sobbing, uncontrollably, like a dam breaking. I realized this was something she never spoke about, kept it locked down, deep in her soul, only to manifest itself in ways she probably didn't even realize. God, I understood that. I pushed off the counter and pulled her into my arms and let her cry. Cry, cry, cry, into my chest while I stroked her hair.

She tilted her head up, the pain in her eyes compared to watching my brothers watch *their* brothers die on the battlefield.

"I saw it..." Her voice pitched with the release of emotions. "I saw her dead body."

She gripped onto my shirt, pulling, and began screaming. Goddammit if tears didn't fill my eyes while I squeezed around her wanting to pull the fury from her and take it as my own. She clenched my shirt, banging her hands against my chest. Then, the short, raspy breaths followed by gasping.

I recognized it instantly.

"Okay, baby," I whispered in her ear. "Don't let it take you. You're okay, take a deep breath." I guided her onto the cold kitchen floor and sat beside her. "Inhale," I whispered, walking her through it. "Exhale... that's it... again." I bent her legs, putting the bottom of each foot on the floor. "Put your head between your legs. Breathe. Focus on the breath. I'm right here."

I stroked her bare back, her skin sizzling to the touch. I closed my eyes and breathed with her, willing her body to relax. Inhale, we breathed together, exhale. Again, and again, until finally, the room went silent. Still.

My finger traced down her spine onto the soft velvet at

her hips. She was so small, vulnerable. So helpless at that moment.

Raw.

Beautiful.

So, *so* beautiful.

She raised her head, the flush gone and an exhausted paleness draining her cheeks. She peered up at me, so sad, so sweet. And with pursed lips and a slight nod, she said *thank you* in her own way. I smiled, dipped my chin, and together we sat on the kitchen floor, two shells of human beings that at one time couldn't be more opposite. At one time, nothing more than a surface level attraction that someone could get in any magazine, any movie. Now, though, there was a deep-rooted understanding, a respect, a ripping away of the armor we'd both built around ourselves. A connection between us, an otherworldly bond. I felt it in the deepest depths of my soul. And it fucking shook me to my core.

I pulled the vodka from the counter and handed it to her. She sipped, then handed it back.

I set it down.

"Better?" My hand stroked her back.

She nodded.

A minute passed.

"How long have you had panic attacks?" I asked.

"Since then."

I nodded, then waited. Waited for the rest of the story because I knew she wasn't done.

"That night, I told the cops everything, every detail I could remember."

"What did they say?"

"About the tattoo? Absolutely nothing. It only took me a few seconds of research to learn that the tattoo was associated with the vicious gang known as the Black V's. I went back to the station and told them, and they said—verbatim—'we'll look into it.' This was right after I'd learned that they'd waited too long to pull the street camera that had recorded the entire thing. The footage had looped. It erases and re-records over every forty-eight hours." Anger flashed. "They waited two days to do something as simple as pull security footage. If they had, there's a good chance the bastards who killed Baba would have been caught."

"How did you know about the camera?"

Her brow tipped up. "I asked around."

"You investigated on your own."

"You're damn right I did, Ax. No one else was, so I took matters into my own hands."

I understood that. More than she even knew at that point.

"It was considered a mugging gone wrong. That was it. It was the hot gossip for a week, then my grandma and her killers were forgotten about, along with every other cold case that was dropped for the next one."

"And then what? What did you do then?"

"I reopened the restaurant. Tripled as the manager, cook, and waitress. Worked my butt off." She smiled. "Baba would've been proud."

"What about your dad? Your brother?"

"Saw them at the funeral. That was it."

"Were they active in the investigation like you were?"

"No." She exhaled. "Then, life went on. I went on, spending every day trying to forget, trying to push the images out of my head. Trying to get a single night's sleep without having nightmares. I learned the 'hot flashes' I'd started having was something called anxiety. Learned the moments I felt like I was being water-boarded was something called panic attacks. I've always blamed myself for not doing something, for not fighting back that night. Not going after them myself." She laughed a humorless laugh. "I can't tell you how many fantasies have played out in my head for if I ever came face to face with the guy again."

"Nothing but a blob of mush, huh?"

A wicked grin crossed her lips. "A dickless ball of mush."

I smiled.

"Anyway, my life had changed, and that horrible night became the past, little by little, until six days ago." She looked at me. "In some twisted act of fate, I've crossed paths with the Black V's again, and, Ax, I won't let this opportunity slip away."

"Erika," I leaned in. "Do you really think it is the same guy? The guy who killed Baba is the same guy who locked you in the cellar?"

"It was the same tattoo, on the forearm. That's all I know, and that's all I need to know. Do you understand that?"

"I do." It was a truthful response. "Where's the ring? The bluebird ring that your grandma gave you?"

"Gone," she seethed through gritted teeth. "Whoever broke into my house the other day took it. It's them. The Black V's are hunting me..." Her eyes narrowed and a tingle swept over my skin. A ball tightened in my gut. I knew that look.

Revenge.

"Erika, listen." I put my hands over hers to refocus her attention, but also in some desperate attempt to pin her to the ground. To keep her from doing what was written all over her face—a kamikaze mission to get revenge for the one love that was taken from her. "You can't go out guns blazing here. These aren't the guys to do that with, you understand? You chase them, you're not coming back—"

"I don't *care,* Ax." The venom spat from her red lips.

"I care. *Dammit.* I care."

We stared at each other for a moment, my heart picking up speed. What the fuck was I saying? Did I mean it? What did I mean, exactly? *Christ.*

I tore my eyes away, pushed off the floor and said, "I get that you don't have faith in law enforcement, Erika, I get it more than you know, trust me. But give this some time." It was all I could think to say to slow her freaking kamikaze roll. "In the meantime, I will make sure nothing happens to you. But I need you to *let me."*

A moment passed.

She looked up at me.

"It's my cross to bear, Ax."

I fell to my knees and grabbed her chin. "It's *ours."*

And I knew, without doubt, that I meant that.

16

ERIKA

I watched the clock click from 6:59am to 7am. *Finally.* I flung the covers off with a frustrated energy that comes only with watching a clock for hours.

Tick, tick, tick, watching the second hand move along the Roman numerals, one after the other, for four freaking hours. The first few hours of my evening had been spent wondering why the Steele brothers had *two* antique ticking clocks in the cabin. Then, I decided that it was probably Ax's idea, because of some medical study he'd read about how the repetitive sound can soothe people who are in duress, as most are when they're under the watchful eye of a personal security firm.

After Ax had picked me up off the floor, he'd drawn me a bath complete with essential oils and candles, and said he'd be 'watching over me' through the night. Whatever that meant. I'd taken an hour-long bath, finishing the bottle of vodka in the process, then paced the little cabin in a desperate attempt to release the restless energy spinning my body. I'd contemplated going for a midnight run, but figured I wouldn't get ten feet before a Steele brother full-body tackled and cuffed me to my bedpost—which, after the vodka, didn't sound half bad. I'd forced myself to lay down sometime after midnight only to further fantasize about Axel Steele and a pair of shiny cuffs.

Two panic attacks in one day, being shot at, and then reliving the most devastating moment of my life was enough to physically drain any human being. Normal human being, anyway. But adding Ax's arms around me, his comfort, his touch, his understanding had sent me into a hormonal induced obsession. I'd laid in bed with my incoherent thoughts shifting between murder and fantasies of what Ax looked like naked.

There was something between us. I could feel it, and I knew he could feel it too. But it was as if neither one of us was willing to acknowledge it. Willing to accept it.

Or maybe that was just me.

You see, for all the sizzling-hot alpha male that was Axel Steele, I had one goal. One goal that deserved all my focus, my attention.

I'd been given a second chance to bring down the group that was responsible for killing my grandmother, and nothing, not even abs of steel—pun intended—or mesmerizing emerald eyes were going to hold me back.

One shot. And I was taking it.

Wearing a long, silk pajama dress—my favorite—I stepped into my pink, fuzzy slippers, padded into the living room and stopped dead in my tracks.

A streak of early morning sunlight glittered through the shaded living room, pooling around a wooden easel, canvas, and chair. On the floor next to it were several boxes, filled with paint.

"Oh my God," I whispered, my mouth gaping.

My eyes darted around the living room, then I jogged to

the kitchen. No Ax. I didn't care, though. I was so happy. *Elated.*

I spun on my heel and walked back to the easel, a smile on my face like a little girl. All my life, I'd never felt a release like when I painted. Nothing, no pill, no drink, no marathon run could take away my anxiety like painting.

It was exactly what I needed.

I traced my finger along the edges, colors already beginning to form on the canvas. I was exploding with creativity, with need to release.

It had been set up in front of the windows, showcasing a mountain landscape worthy of its own frame. I admired the bright orange, yellow, and deep fuchsia shooting up from the horizon. Then, like a magnet, my gaze turned to a silhouette in front of the tree line.

Ax.

A smile crossed my face at the mere sight of him, a tingle of happiness I hadn't felt in a long time.

Maybe ever.

I watched him raise the ax in his hand, then with a *crack,* split a massive log in two. In every bit of my alpha-male fantasy the night before, he wore a red plaid shirt over a grey t-shirt. Dirty jeans and combat boots, and a SIG secured to his belt.

I stepped onto the deck, the cool, crisp morning air like a shot of espresso.

He looked up, the light catching his face, a smile catching his lips.

I smiled back and placed my hands on the rail. "Who chops wood at seven in the morning?"

"Who wears *that* to sleep in?"

I grinned and watched him split one last log, then secure the ax into the stump. After wiping the sweat from his brow, he stepped across the lawn and looked up at me, high above in my princess balcony.

"Good morning."

"Indeed. Ax, how did you know? More importantly, how did you sneak it in?"

"Stealth is kind of my thing."

"Special ops, got it." The thought of Ax sneaking round the cabin during my few hours of rest should have creeped me out. But it had the opposite effect—it comforted me. *He* comforted me. And I liked it.

I leaned over the railing, my body wanting to close the ten feet between us. "Seriously, how did you know?"

His gaze shifted to my chest, spilling out of my dress, and a wave of sexual awareness flew over me.

"Can I come up?" He asked, heat simmering in those green eyes.

"Of course."

I unlocked the front door, jogged to the kitchen and put coffee on to brew. Then, I darted to the bathroom and brushed my teeth with the vigor of someone who hadn't seen a toothbrush in years. I ran my fingers through my hair as the door opened. After giving myself a once-over and deciding it would have to do, I stepped into the living room where Ax was stacking wood on an iron grate next to the fireplace. He smelled of fresh air and cedar.

My stomach tickled.

"Starting a fire?"

"Loading up for winter."

"You cut your own wood?"

He sent me a confused glance. Because, why wouldn't he? Of course the Steele brothers cut their own firewood. Duh. They probably ate off the land and drank from the streams too... in nothing but scraps of fur covering their privates.

Okay, I needed to get laid.

"The main house is an energy sucker," he continued. "Costs a lot to heat. We use the fireplaces as much as possible."

Because nothing was more soothing than a crackling fire on a cold, wintry night. And suddenly, I wanted nothing else in the world more than that. With him, on the couch.

"You like it?" He cleared his throat and stood.

"I love it." I looked back at the easel. "I can't believe... I mean, how did you know I painted?"

"Well, there was the Mona Lisa T-shirt you were wearing when you got here, the Starry Night tattoo on your arm, and the Water Lily Pond bag you had in the bathroom. Da Vinci, Van Gogh, Monet... Zajac." He winked.

My heart swelled. "You noticed all that?"

"Pay attention, remember?"

"Just part of the job, huh?"

His eyes twinkled as they narrowed. "Part of the job."

The coffee pot dinged with the electricity shooting between us.

"Want some?" I asked.

He perused my chest again and I felt the heat rise up my body. One thing was for sure, Ax Steele did all sorts of things to my sympathetic system. Or whatever the hell it was called.

"More than anything." He said as his eyes met mine.

Sexual innuendo. Check.

I could feel his eyes burning into me as he followed me into the kitchen, and dammit if my hips didn't have a little extra sway in them. A mind of their own, those things.

I grabbed two mugs from the cabinet and filled each.

"Creamer?"

"Black."

Of course.

I handed him his, then wrapped both hands around mine and leaned against the counter. "So, what time did you sneak into my cabin?"

He sipped, watching me over the rim. "You were up late, Miss Zajac."

My brow cocked. "You were watching me."

"My job."

"Thorough."

"Trained."

The phone on his hip dinged and he glanced at the clock, then back at me.

"How are you? This morning?" He asked, ignoring the phone.

"It's..." I shook my head and looked out the window. "A lot."

"I know."

Our eyes met, and for a moment, we stared at each other.

He sipped again, then said, "Detective Jagger is planning to come out and speak with you this morning about last night, along with an FBI agent named Olivia Mackenzie."

"I figured. I'm ready."

"Listen, I want you to tell them everything. About the tattoo, even your thoughts about how law enforcement failed you in the past. *Everything.*"

I sipped, a ball forming in my stomach.

He watched me for a second, then said, "I've got to run into town this morning, and have a few things I need to get done today."

"Besides chopping wood?"

"Right." He looked at the clock again. "Celeste will be here in three minutes to take you on a jog."

"*Take* me on a *jog?*"

He nodded.

"I can take myself, thank you very much."

"I have no doubt you can, but she's going to accompany you today—"

I opened my mouth—

"It's not negotiable, Erika. You're going, and Celeste is going with you. End of discussion."

"You're trying to keep me busy."

"Busy is always good."

This from the guy who never slept and chopped wood at daybreak.

"Maybe I don't want to jog."

"Maybe you need to work on your lying skills."

My brows tipped up. "Fine. How do you know I'm a jogger?"

He slowly scanned my body, sweeping over every inch with the heat of a thousand suns.

"Let me guess, because you remember I was out jogging when I found the cellar, and the jogging shoes in my bag..."

"Pay—"

"Attention. Got it."

He grinned, then glanced at the clock for the third time. The guy had somewhere he needed to be, but something was keeping him from walking out that door.

I glanced over my shoulder at the painting easel, now glowing with dawn's early light, then back at him. He was definitely trying to keep me busy and I wasn't sure if it was to keep me from hunting the Black V's by myself, or from having another panic attack when he wasn't around... or, perhaps both.

"A hike through the woods, painting... I'll try to relax, I promise."

He said nothing, just stared back.

"What if it doesn't work?" I asked.

Heat flashed in his eyes. "Then I've got another idea."

With that, he set down his coffee, crossed the room and kissed my forehead, leaving the skin tingling and my stomach dancing as he pulled away.

"Be good," he said as he crossed the cabin. And to further demonstrate Ax's infallible punctuality, Celeste pulled up the driveway the moment he walked out the front door.

17

AXEL

*A*ntiseptic and bleach. The smell was like a punch in the face when I walked through the sliding glass doors and was met with a wall of ice-cold air and a sobbing woman with her head buried in her husband's chest.

I fucking hated hospitals. And not only the smell, the food, it was the cloying desperation that hung in the air like a thick, wet blanket. A constant dark cloud hellbent on blocking the light of hope to enter any room. I had hope, sure, but it was wrapped in layers and layers of rage. The same feeling I felt every time I stepped into a hospital, except this time, the anger was amped up a few billion percent.

My brothers and I were fix-it-yourself kind of guys, a notion sealed in stone the first time our dad asked Phoenix to sew his eyebrow shut after a branch had fallen on him one winter day. With no medical training whatsoever, our father calmly walked my brother through stitching a gaping wound on his own head. A week later, while chopping firewood, I hit a knot in a log causing the ax to bounce back and split my chin. After I'd blinked the stars from my eyes, I stumbled my way back to the house, locked myself in the bathroom and with nothing but a bottle of rubbing alcohol, needle, and ball of surgical sutures, I stitched myself up, stopping three different times to throw up. I was nine years old. After that, we took care of each other, me being the go-to medical advisor of the family, of course. Only the rarest of cases where one of us needed a prescription for something, did we call in our old friend Dr. Buckley, a family practice doctor who still believed in bedside manner and house calls. My brothers and I did everything in our power to avoid clinics and hospitals. We didn't believe in weakness. We didn't believe in needing someone else to do for us that, technically, we could do ourselves. Even if it wasn't the smartest move. Doctors over-diagnosed and over-medicated, an issue that ran rampant within the military and with veterans. I had a very intimate relationship with PTSD, as did most of my brothers in special ops. But we toughed it out. Manned up. Why? Because more often than not the answer to PTSD was to "take this pill in the morning, this pill at lunch, and this pill in the evening." Endless refills. Enjoy.

Screw. That.

No, we avoided doctors at all cost.

Call it macho, whatever, but to four guys who'd spent their lives in war zones, hospitals were a sign of doom.

Of death.

And never had I felt the grim reaper at my doorstep as I did that day.

I cursed the ball twisting in my gut as I walked down the blinding white hall.

God, I *hated* hospitals.

I paused at the last door on the right, inhaled, then slowly pushed it open.

Dallas looked over from the smudged window she'd been staring out of.

"Ax," she smiled and pushed herself to a stance, a little unsteady on her feet. My stepmother was one of the most badass females I'd ever met. The woman was the picture of in-control, never showing real emotions, never backing down from a fight. She was a strong, southern woman with a brain like a computer. Dad always told me I'd gotten my book smarts from her, and street smarts from him. She was a woman who always had it all together, from her perfectly coiffed blonde hair to her freshly manicured nails, to the impeccable makeup she wore that made her appear a decade younger that her forty-three years.

But not that day. That day, Dallas Steele was as pale as the pillow she'd stacked behind her back. Her hair was pulled back in a messy bun, matching her over-sized, wrinkled T-shirt and jeans. Cracks beginning to show after a year of losing her husband and now, potentially her stepson, who she'd raised since he was a young boy.

I crossed the room and she stepped into my open arms. As she squeezed, I peeked at my brother from the corner of my eye.

An image that still made my heart drop to my feet.

Drains flowed from his bandaged head like a robotic version of Medusa. A feeding tube protruded from his stomach. Dozens of wires attached to his torso. IV's ran from both arms, connecting to metal stands with multiple bags.

The *beep, beep, beep* of his heart monitor inciting more jitters in me than gunfire edging closer to my team's location.

Dallas released me and crossed her arms over her chest.

We both turned toward Phoenix.

"How is he today?"

"Same."

A minute passed.

Dallas exhaled, turned to back me. "How are things at the house?"

"Go find out for yourself. Sleep, Mama, have a drink, relax. Play the piano, watch some reality TV, whatever. Go. I've got this."

She smiled, squeezed my shoulder. "You, Ax, you were always the one to take care of your brothers."

"No, Dallas, that's you. Dad was always gone. If not for you, we wouldn't have had any parents. Which, Gage might've actually liked."

She snorted. "That boy. No, Ax, you always see the bigger picture." She tapped my forehead. "But sometimes, you need to give those wheels of yours a rest."

"I will, Ma—you first."

She nodded, shifted to where she was in front of the small mirror that hung above the sink. "I do need a shower, don't I?"

"Well, I wasn't going to say anything..." I winked, kissed her cheek. "Git."

"Yes, sir." She gathered her overnight designer bag and purse. "Who's next?"

"Gunner will be here in four hours to release me, then you're scheduled for another four hours after that."

"So I've got eight hours."

"Plenty of time to get shnockered, pass out, sleep it off, and sober up again." I smirked.

"Doesn't sound half bad." She paused, narrowed her eyes. "I heard about the Fall Harvest Party. How's Cabin 2?"

"Pain in my ass."

She laughed. "They all are."

After stepping past me, she glanced over her shoulder, "Don't overthink it, son."

Four hours later I drove my Harley up the long driveway that led to the main house. The afternoon had grown overcast with the promise of rain. The depressing bleak sky stealing the vivid colors of fall, leaving nothing but drab, flaking leaves pitifully falling from the trees. There was a feeling of doom, foreboding, in the cool air whipping around my leather jacket. It was like death was all around me. Like the world had finally succumbed to it.

I felt like I'd run a marathon through the Sahara Desert. The energy depletion of sitting in the ICU was second only to being in the middle of a war zone. It wasn't just the hospital, it was staring at my oldest brother, my hero since I was a baby, incapacitated and fighting for his life. Watching every shallow inhale of his breath, praying it wasn't the last. Wondering if it were, did he have a good life? Did Feen die happy? Was I a good brother? And then, the regrets... god*damn* the regrets. Thinking of our last conversation, our last argument. Why did I say that, when I could have said it differently? Guilt—now that's an unrelenting bitch that destroys you from the inside out. Memories of our childhood flashed through my head like projected clips behind a eulogy.

Did I mention I hated hospitals?

Somewhere into hour two, I forced the thoughts of death aside, and instead shifted my focus to Feen pulling through.

What would his life be like?

Could he talk? Move? Reason? Would he be banished to live the rest of his days as a vegetable, the unstoppable hands of time aging his lifeless body against nothing but cotton sheets and a mechanical bed.

The thought was unbearable. For him. I knew, without the shadow of a doubt that Feen would rather die than drool his life away.

Would we have to make that decision?

Could we?

Hope.

Life was nothing without it. I knew that, perhaps I was the only Steele brother who knew that.

Mind over matter, I kept telling myself as I sat there in ICU, staring at my brother.

Mind over matter.

I forced myself into my comfort zone, analyzing the days and moments around his incident. And for every scenario I'd come up with, one thing was definite—If Phoenix Steele had wanted to commit suicide, he would have done it.

Period.

He would have done it with fucking gusto, leaving no stone unturned to guarantee his eyes would be shut forever. Feen wouldn't have shot himself at an angle. No, Feen would have shoved the gun into his mouth and pulled the trigger.

Someone had tried to kill my brother. Even if the small-town, small-minded cops didn't think so.

I thought of Erika, and her lack of faith in law enforcement.

I got it. I understood.

I understood that woman.

And I understood that both of us, at that moment in time, were consumed with one thing—revenge.

While I stared at a broken piece of my soul laying there in the hospital bed, one thing became clear as day to me. I couldn't lose her, too. With my brother holding on by a string, I couldn't lose her on top of that.

The morning had been a total mind fuck from top to bottom, and although it was only noon, I wanted nothing more than a handle of Johnnie Walker Blue.

I rolled to a stop in front of the house and turned off the engine. The *pop, pop, pop* of gunfire in the distance told me that Gage had taken Gunner's place at the shooting range. After pushing through the front door, I jogged up the grand staircase and headed down the hall to our main security room.

Wearing his usual ripped jeans, T-shirt and flip-flops, Wolf sat behind the command center with multiple computer monitors in front of a wall of televisions, each flipping through the dozens of security cameras we had throughout the property. Only the glow of the screens and a dim floor lamp lit the room.

Wolf didn't move. I wasn't even sure if he'd heard me come in. He was engrossed in a tiny code running across one of the screens.

"Anything new?" I crossed the room, still unsure if he'd heard me. "Yo, *Wolf.*"

Finally I got a grunt, his eyes never leaving the screen.

"*Hey.*" I snapped. "I just got back from the hospital and am not in the mood, bro."

Wolf cocked a brow, gave me the once-over, then focused back on the screen while grabbing a beer from the mini-fridge at his feet. He popped the top and handed it to me.

"Drink." He said.

I did. And it felt good.

"Better?"

I exhaled and rolled my eyes.

"Good. Sit. Okay... the Knight Fox, the dude who we think killed your dad and tried to kill Phoenix..."

"You find him yet?"

"Not yet. Getting closer though."

"Whatya got?"

"Okay, so thanks to Feen's tireless investigating before, you know, we know that your wicked smart dad was secretly researching the assassination of Andrei Sokolov, a big dick in the Russian KGB, in the days before his death, right?"

"Right. And two days before Dad died, he uncovered a code embedded into our satellite system that correlates to the exact date that Sokolov was murdered."

"Indicating someone here in the US was involved in arranging the hit..."

"And didn't want anyone to know about it."

"Exactly. So, Feen dives head first into this shit, and discovers that someone named the Knight Fox is not only involved, but was here in Berry Springs the day your dad died."

"Was murdered, Wolf. The Fox murdered Dad when he started digging too deep into this secret code, and then tried to kill Feen when he reopened pandora's box."

"By appearances, yes."

"Not appearances, Wolf, screw you. The Knight Fox did this. You know that."

"Dude." He slid me the side eye. "Drink your damn drink."

"Fine." I chugged. "Fine. Sorry. Go on."

"Are you sure, because now *I'm* not in the mood..."

"Go *on.*"

He stared at me a moment, one brow cocked before blowing out a breath and turning back to the screen.

"Your dad was researching quantum cryptography, specifically QKD, or quantum key distribution."

"I know what QKD is, Wolf."

He laughed. "Sorry, Gage was just here."

I grinned.

"So then you know that it's essentially a set of keys—in this case, sent via satellite—that is used as a password to unlock a form of communication. It's an almost untraceable way to send confidential information—very, very confidential information."

"Such as sending hit information on Andrei Sokolov."

"Right. Anything. So to understand how your dad got into trouble here, you need to understand how it works. QKD is literally an infallible way to send encryption. It's carried through a photon, which is an element. A photon can't be copied, but better than that, if there's any attempt to intercept, say by *your dad*, it disturbs the photon, leaving an obvious change in its pattern. Whoever created the key knows it was messed with. It's genius, really. It's a huge advancement in cybersecurity... and for any evil-doer wanting to send secret messages anywhere in the world." He glanced at me. "Side note, it will also make spying on other countries difficult. Primed for controversy, this is. But we won't go into that right now."

I ran my fingers through my hair. "And Dad was heading up the team researching quantum cryptography at the NSA."

"Yep." He turned to me. "You really think someone from the NSA killed him? That the US was involved in the Russian assassination, your dad found out about it, and was killed for it?"

"Can't ignore the possibility. And that's where you and

your freakish love for hacking comes in. What else have you found, Wolf?"

"Okay," he rubbed his hands together with a spurt of excitement. "So you know that your dad had hacked into Sokolov's email and tracked a few emails signed *KF* to a burner phone that bounced off a local tower here in Berry Springs. Well, that wasn't all I found in the emails. Sokolov's bodyguard, who we can assume was in on killing Sokolov, had wired money to an offshore account—"

"Let me guess, here in the US."

"Bingo."

"Tell me you've got the name of the account holder."

"Of course not. The company was set up seventeen years ago, anonymously. To date, nine point two million dollars have funneled through it."

"You're kidding. From where?"

"An account linked to *another* shell company, but this one has a name. H and S Star Incorporated."

"H and S Star..." I repeated. "Do we know what it stands for?"

"Nope."

"H and S Star..." I muttered, my mind racing. "*Wait.* The connection here is Russia, right? Andrei Sokolov was the start to all this."

"That's right."

I snorted, shook my head. "H and S... Hammer and sickle, Wolf. Freakin' hammer and sickle."

His eyes rounded. "The old soviet flag."

I scrubbed my hands over my face. "Yep."

"Nice work, detective Steele." He focused back on the screen. "Well, I hope you speak Russian."

I pulled my hands down from my face. "Why?"

"Because there is a single cell phone linked to H and S."

"You're kidd—wait, have you tracked it? Where is it? Who's is it?"

"Slow down there, Ace. The phone has been turned off since I discovered it. I only have the number."

"It hasn't been turned on?"

"Nope."

"Not once?"

"Nope."

"There's no log of any information you can pull from it?"

"Nope."

I began pacing. "Let's recap here. The Knight Fox is here in the US, quite possibly here in Berry Springs, and is receiving payment from Russia for something. It's a freaking secret spy, Wolf. The Fox is a Russian spy."

"A Russian spy who killed your dad and tried to kill your brother."

My blood pumped like a firehose through my neck. "It could be anyone, Wolf. It could be someone in the government, someone who worked with Dad at the NSA."

"Agreed. That's what they do, they embed themselves into our society, become one of us, sometimes for years, decades, before they strike."

"We can't trust anyone, Wolf."

"No. We can't, and the worst part is, it could be any one of us. Anyone. *Anyone,* Ax. We don't know anything about the Knight Fox. We don't have anything on him."

"Yes we do. We've got his number, Wolf. And that's something." My thoughts reeled as I turned toward the door.

"Hey, Ax?"

"Yeah?"

"One more thing. Gunner asked me to look into Cabin 2's brother, his company..."

I stopped cold. "And?"

"Thought you'd want to know that Zajac Investments is about to file bankruptcy."

"What?"

"Yep. That Filip cat has been selling stocks, homes, cars, to try to keep it going."

My brows tipped up.

Zajac Investments was in financial trouble.

Erika wasn't the only Zajac with secrets.

18

ERIKA

I dipped the brush in orange, dabbed a bit of yellow and streaked the canvas in front of me. Soft, slow strokes. My gaze flittered to the soaring mountains outside the window, the black clouds in the distance, capping a grey sky that had been threatening rain all day. True to the season, the weather was unapologetically unpredictable with temperatures dipping into the high fifties that afternoon. Combining that with the steady breeze, it felt even cooler. I'd pulled a sweater over my t-shirt and had settled in to paint in an attempt to escape, if even for a few hours. An attempt to distract my thoughts from both the Black V's *and* Ax Steele, a force as powerful as the V's, apparently.

Keeping my eyes on the painting, I plucked my glass of wine from the floor and sipped. It certainly wasn't five, but I didn't give a shit.

My head tilted as I stared at my picture, my creation, and noticed a difference from my usual paintings. Everything from the colors I'd chosen, the streaks, the feel of it. It was darker, sadder, more emotional than anything I'd painted before.

An impending doom, coming out of me, right there onto the canvas.

I sipped, then sloshed the wine as a knock rapped on the door.

"Dammit." I darted to the kitchen and after dabbing the sure-to-be-a-stain on my beige sweater, I padded across the living area and opened the front door, and smiled.

"Hey."

"Hey." Ax smiled back but even those lips couldn't distract from the aura of stress around him.

"Come in."

He stepped inside and looked down at the red dots on my sweater.

"I told Celeste to take you up the mountain, not the bar."

"And this is what happened when she wouldn't take me to the bar."

The corner of his lip curled up and it felt like a little victory.

"Stitches?"

"Only a few. She's recovering nicely."

"Never come between Erika and her bar. Note to self."

I licked my fingers and dabbed the stains. I liked that sweater.

"You scared me. Didn't expect you."

"Whoa." He locked onto my painting as he beelined it across the room.

Insecurity washed over me, surprising me. Why did I care what he thought?

"That's..." he looked back at me with widened eyes. "Amazing. It's beautiful, Erika."

I wrinkled my nose, gazing at the picture of the angry sunset in front of me.

"It's not my best work."

"Not your *best* work?"

"Yeah..." I pinched my lips. "It's different than I usually paint. Darker."

He shook his head, still staring at the canvas as if it were the hope diamond. "No..." he pointed. "See here? The light. You found the light."

I focused on the bright streak of yellow I'd painted literally seconds before he'd walked in—a golden beam in the angry sky. A single beam of light penetrating the darkness.

"You're crazy talented."

He got the crazy part right. I smiled, glanced down.

"Seriously, Erika." He said, his enthusiasm making me both elated and embarrassed. "You should do this as a job. You're very talented."

My smile widened, because I couldn't help it. I took a step back. I knew I was a good artist, I'd have to be blind not to, but I'd never been good at receiving compliments. They always made me a bit itchy.

"So, anyway," I said, eager to change the subject. "What brings you here this afternoon, or early evening, I should say? Besides the art."

He shifted his weight, his brows knitted as he looked down. He'd had a heck of a day, and I wanted to make it better. To see that smile again.

More than that, I didn't want him to leave. So, I said, "I think there's still a few drops of wine left that didn't make it onto my sweater."

"I had something else in mind."

My brow cocked.

"A walk."

"A walk?"

"Yeah, an act of traveling on foot, more often than not for pleasure."

I had a few other ideas that involved pleasure, but I let that slide. And chocked it up to the wine—on my shirt.

"A walk, where?"

"The woods."

I looked out the window, where, ironically, a few beams of sunlight cut through the dense cloud cover.

"I could use some fresh air," he said mindlessly, following my gaze.

"Me, too. I'll grab my jacket."

After quadruple locking the cabin, we started down a windy pebbled pathway into the woods. The air was crisp, cool, clean, perfumed with the spicy scent of fall. Pine needles and dead leaves crunched under the hiking boots I'd slipped over my ripped skinny jeans. In contrast to my wine-dotted sweater and jacket, Ax was in a black T-shirt that clung to his muscular chest, and jeans that clung to that ass that made me want to giggle.

I watched him for a moment, the hard set of his jaw, the intensity in his eyes. Ax always had a general pissed-off look about him, but this was different.

"What's going on, Ax?"

He glanced at me. "... Nothing."

"Not nothing. Something's up."

No response.

"I'm paying attention."

He smiled, but still avoided the question. We walked a few yards in silence, a comfortable silence, listening to the nature around us, breathing in the fresh mountain air. We both were in our element, and we both knew it.

"How did today go?" He asked.

"The jog with Celeste was good. It felt good. So... thank you for that. And getting back behind a canvas again... thank you for that, too."

"Celeste told me you met with Jagg and an Agent Mackenzie with the FBI."

"I did. For about forty-five minutes. Re-capped the party, everything that happened."

"Did you tell them about your grandma, the tattoo, the ring?"

"They know the ring is missing. I sent the list of the jewelry that was taken to the cops. They have that; they have everything."

"And about your grandma?"

"They *know*, Ax. They said they read the file. They know." I shook my head, frustration beginning to boil up. "Do you know anything that I don't? Is there anything new? Have they found anything in the cellar?"

"Jessa Watson's DNA is all over the place, and yours, too, but so far nothing from the suspect. Same with your house. Whoever broke in wore gloves. Knew what he was doing. They're still filtering through the vehicles that came and left the park in the days surrounding your incident."

"What about the Fall Harvest Party? Are they comparing the vehicles that were there?"

"None match."

"What about where the guy shot from?"

"Nothing."

I released a frustrated groan.

"There's also no connection to the victims, nothing linking them together."

"Except for their proximity to me."

He nodded.

"The guy's not a good shot."

"He's desperate. Desperation makes you messy."

I snorted. "I understand messy, trust me."

He glanced over, watched me a moment. "No panic attacks today?"

I shook my head, looked away.

"Hey. Don't be embarrassed."

"Says the guy who's saved my life twice now. Says the guy who's always on the ball, always *paying attention*."

He didn't say anything, just walked next to me, listening as I continued. "It's humiliating. And side note, scary, too. It's like it completely takes over my body. I hate it, Ax."

"How often do you get them?"

"Less now."

"Did you see a doctor?"

"Eventually, yes."

"Eventually?"

I took a deep breath. "I denied it for a while, was embarrassed. Thought the attacks meant I was a weak person. But then, one night, I was out with a few of my girlfriends, having drinks. I called it a night around eleven or so—you know, six in the morning for you…"

He smirked.

"Because you don't ever sleep—"

"I got it. Keep going."

"Anyway, I had to walk to my car. A road was closed for construction, so I had to take an alley to the parking lot where I'd parked. It was dark, the dumpsters, a cluster of trees at the other end… it reminded me of that night."

"And you had an attack right there?"

I nodded. "A group of teenagers found me, gasping for air, flailing on the ground like an idiot. They carried me into a nearby gas station and got me some water, freaking called an ambulance."

"Oh God."

"I know. Within three minutes, it was a circus. I had to explain to everyone that it was nothing but a stupid panic attack and for everyone to go home." I laughed a humorless laugh. "You want to know the funniest part? The full amount of embarrassment didn't hit me until I got home. I was wearing a silk top with these light grey slacks—"

"Gucci?"

I smirked. "Diane von Furstenberg. Anyway, panic attacks make you sweat, right? So when I got home, I went into the bathroom to take an ice-cold shower and noticed my clothes were soaked. My arm pits were saturated, and when I turned around, I had these perfect rings under each butt cheek—sweat rings that looked like I'd peed myself. It's ridiculous, but that was what sent me over the edge. All those people thought I'd wet myself. The teenage kids, the paramedics, everyone going in and out of the gas station. It was like, okay, panic attack, you not only took my confidence, you took every shred of dignity I had. So, yeah, I made an appointment with a doctor that week—right after I received the nine-hundred dollar ambulance bill that I didn't even ride in."

"And what did he say?"

"She. Women are doctors too, you know."

He grinned. "Sorry. What did *she* say?"

"PTSD."

His neck snapped to me, something flashing in his eyes, and I knew that he knew all about PTSD.

"Related to what happened with your grandma?"

"Yep. All those years later, everything was from that single incident."

"PTSD can last for years, decades, sometimes someone's entire life. Did they put you on pills?"

"Oh, yeah. Two different kinds."

He shook his head.

"I took them for about three years, then decided I didn't like it. Didn't like something that altered me so much. My brain, specifically. One day, I decided that I was going to overcome it. Naturally. So, I tossed the pills down the toilet—"

"You're not supposed to do that."

"Do what?"

"Toss prescription drugs down the toilet. It pollutes and contaminates food and water supplies."

"Thanks, Michelangelo."

"Was Michelangelo an environmentalist?"

"No, he was really smart. Knew a little about everything. Had an IQ of almost two hundred or something." I cocked my head. "I'm surprised you didn't know this."

He grinned. "Go on..."

I laughed. "As I was saying, so—after polluting food and water supplies—I sought out relaxation in other ways that didn't involve drugs. Painting, running, fitness, yoga, meditating..."

"Tattoos?"

"No, I started getting these after I moved out from my dad's house. Call it rebellion, whatever, but honestly, I felt like I was finally, after sixteen years, coming into my own."

"What was your first one?"

"Cassiopeia."

Our eyes locked for a split-second.

"Anyway, so painting, running, yoga, meditating, *vodka,* all helped me relax."

"So is that where this boho hippie thing comes from?"

"Boho hippie thing?"

"You've got an earthy vibe to you, one-with-nature sort of

thing." He reached over and flicked one of the thin braids I had running over my hair.

"Thanks?"

"I like it."

We walked a moment in silence, then, he said, "What I don't get is that someone who is usually 'one with nature,' is not into labels and material things."

"What makes you think I'm into *labels*?"

"Well, your luggage for one. Louis Vuitton, and those diamond stud earrings you wear in your ears. The Valentino dress you wore to the party. Half your bag was designer shoes... and then there's that silk dress thing you had on this morning—"

"Those were pajamas. My jammies."

"Jammies?"

I slid him the side-eye. "That's right."

"I'll let that one go. Anyway, it looked expensive."

"I like nice things." I motioned in the direction of his uber-mansion. "Pot calling the kettle black."

"Hey, no judgment, I like nice things, too. But what I'm saying is that it doesn't add up. Most of our clients have money, and the list of things they request within an hour of being booked into a cabin is endless. Celeste hates it. They gripe about this, about that, the type of wine we have—the whole nine yards. Not you though, you didn't ask for a single thing. And according to Celeste, you're one of the few. You've got a few expensive things, but the majority of the things you wear are worn thin with holes or stains."

"Damn the wine."

"Don't deflect."

I cleared my throat knowing where this was going, and, honestly, surprised that it had taken him so long to ask.

He continued, "You told us that you have no part in your

brother's company, you aren't on his payroll, and don't accept handouts. Didn't mention an early inheritance. You haven't mentioned any other job since working at the restaurant decades ago. Yet, according to your social media account, you travel the world and it doesn't appear that you're backpacking. So, Erika, tell me... what is it that you do for a living?"

"Where do I make the money to buy all my fancy-schmancy things?"

"Answer the question."

My stomach knotted.

He helped me over a fallen log, and we walked a few more steps in silence.

"I paint." I said finally, forcing the word out.

His brows tipped up. "This, I can see. For how long?"

"My whole life, but I started selling them about fifteen years ago. Right around the time I realized I wouldn't be able to run a restaurant and pay rent at the same time."

"You must sell a lot of paintings."

I smiled, because I couldn't fight it. Because I was proud.

Assessing me, he said, "You sell a lot, don't you."

I glanced away, feeling his fixation burning into me.

"Who are you, Erika?"

I heaved out an exhale. "You know that painting you have next to your staircase?"

His eyes popped. "You're Agatha *Rose*?"

I spread my hands. "Pleasure to meet you."

He stopped in his tracks and turned to me. "You're *kidding* me."

"Nope." I shifted my weight.

"Another one of your paintings hangs in my *dad's* office, Erika. The one of the geese flying over the sunset. He loved it. I remember when he bought it—Holy *shit,* at a *really* exclusive art auction."

I looked down again.

"Erika, you're legitimately famous."

"No, *I'm* not—panic-attacking, daughter-of-an-immigrant Erika Zajac is not famous. Agatha Rose is."

He watched me for a minute, his mouth gaping. "Why? Why keep it a secret? Why hide? You're so talented. You must know it."

"I do, and thank you. When I decided I was going to try to sell my art, I wasn't sure if it would sell. Honestly, I worried that people would laugh at it. And if they did, I didn't want to bring shame to my grandma. So, I tacked a fake name to it, and to my shock, things kind of took off. I decided to keep the name because I didn't want to have to *be* the brand, be out in public."

"Because of the panic attacks."

I nodded. It was one-hundred percent true. And that embarrassed me.

"You can't let that take over your life."

There was something in his tone that told me he was talking about more than the panic attacks. I needed to let the Black V's go, too.

I sighed and peered up at the dark clouds moving swiftly through the sky. A trio of orange leaves flittered down from the trees. "I know. I've just... I've never had anyone remind me of that."

He stared at me with an intensity that had my stomach flipping. A gust of wind swept between us, sending leaves swirling around us.

Butterflies burst in my stomach.

His gaze slid down to my mouth.

Kiss me, I thought. Dear, God, *kiss me.*

But instead, being typical Ax, that brain of his went into overdrive and he took a step back, dropping the temperature around my body about twenty degrees.

He turned away, and started walking.

I caught up, and changed the subject. "Well, that was my big secret reveal, now it's your turn. Tell me about your day."

He suddenly stopped again, his gaze locking on a massive, old oak tree with snarled branches weaving around bright yellow leaves. It was a painting all itself and I half expected it to start talking and sprinkling fairy dust.

He was lost in it, his face hardening, eyes squinting.

Pain.

"Tell me, I said."

"My brother," he said almost breathlessly. "Phoenix, my older brother, and I would climb this tree almost every day when we were growing up." His jaw clenched with emotion. "I remember him challenging me, taunting me, that I couldn't make it to the top before he could... I always let him win. Besides," he looked at me, a crooked grin, "a broken arm wouldn't serve me well in football practice the next morning."

"Always thinking."

"That's right. We'd sit in it for hours, Phoenix carving into the trunk... hell, I think he even fell asleep in it a few times. Me, I'd sit there with him, either watching the birds, squirrels, the clouds come in. Or, I'd read. Whatever 'weird-ass' book I'd chosen that week. Feen's words, not mine."

A moment passed.

"Gage was always out chasing ass, and Gunner always either working on some bullshit in the garage or shooting his BB gun. But me and Feen would come here. ... *Damn,*" he bit his lip, lost in memories. "He gave me my first beer in that damn tree." His voice cracked, and I swore I saw the glint of a tear in his eyes.

He turned his back to me, took a few steps, then inhaled and tilted his head to the sky. "Storm's rolling in."

"Tell me, Ax. What happened?"

A solid minute passed before the man with emotional armor thicker than the wall he'd built around himself launched into the story of his brother clinging to life at the local ICU. I stood frozen to the ground listening to the words pour out of him as if a dam had finally broken. Watching him sway between grief, sadness, and a volcanic rage that shook me to my very core.

After the story was over, he shoved his hands into his pocket, keeping his back to me. I knew the feeling. He was embarrassed. Embarrassed that he bared himself to me.

My heart sitting in a million pieces on the forest floor, I walked up to him, wrapped my arms around his waist and rested my cheek on his back.

His hand slid over mine.

And then, it started to rain.

19

ERIKA

*W*e burst through the front door of Cabin 2 with me giggling like a little girl as I slid across the hardwood floor. Ax caught me—per usual—and steadied me. Lightning flashed through the dark room, followed by a crash of thunder.

"We're *soaked.*" Chest heaving, I wiped the water streaming down my face. Ax ran his fingers through his hair, droplets of water falling onto my face.

The sprinkles had turned into a deluge within minutes, soaking us to the bone as we jogged back to the cabin. The temperature had dropped at least ten degrees with the rain, the clouds darkening the early evening as if it were already midnight.

Ax wiped his muddy boots on the mat and I took a second to marvel at the way the wet T-shirt clung to his chest. The guy had bowling balls for shoulders and, dear Lord, I wanted to take them for a spin.

"I'll get us some towels," I said instead and disappeared into the bedroom. When I came out, he'd busied himself by stacking logs into the fireplace.

He ignored the towel I'd set down beside him and kept stacking. I couldn't get a read on him. He was quiet, stoic almost, and I guessed it was because he wasn't used to baring his soul to anyone, especially to a woman.

So, I did the only thing I could think of. Grabbed us both a glass of wine.

"Thank you for getting a fire started." I handed him a man-sized glass.

He nodded, sipped—make that *chugged* half the glass—then focused on the kindling in the fire. Something was up with him, no doubt about that.

"I'm going to go change."

Another silent nod, zero eye contact. One minute the guy was about to kiss me, then he clammed up, only to open up to me emotionally, then lock up again like a safe. And I thought *I* was a rollercoaster.

I closed the bathroom door and after peeling off my sopping wet clothes, I toweled off and examined my naked body in the mirror.

I wanted him. In the most intimate way.

I wanted to hold him, for him to hold me. I wanted everything from him, if only for one night.

I wanted to feel that power, that intensity that was Ax, inside me, because something told me it was a one shot deal. No other man on earth was like Axel Steele.

Seize the moment, I thought.

All we ever have is right now.

I sipped my wine, my gaze shifting to the long, black, silk night gown hanging in the closet that seemed to hypnotize him earlier. A smile curved my lips, and after dabbing a touch of perfume behind my ears, I slipped it on.

Doing the equivalent of a manly thump on my chest, I

took a deep breath, and after downing my wine, I stepped out of the bathroom.

~

Axel

I wanted to curse, spit, run my motor cycle into a tree, bash my head through the rock fireplace in front of me.

I was a mess.

A fucking mess.

I didn't know what had come over me when I'd told Erika about my brother, getting all emotional like a damn pussy. I'd never opened up like that.

To anyone.

Not to my dad, to Dallas, to my brothers. No one.

I'd had to suck back tears toward the end, for Christ's sake. Then, by the glory of the Gods, the heavens above opened up and rained down on us, interrupting my girly-ass mental break and preserving the single shred of testosterone I had left.

What did Erika think of me now?

Who the hell wanted an emotional basket case as a bodyguard, or hell, anything else for that matter?

I'd start her a fire, I'd decided, then hit the shooting range with Gunner until the sun came up, regaining the masculinity that I'd left right there in the woods.

I was *off*.

And I fucking hated that.

I needed something. Something to pin down the firestorm spiraling through my veins.

I needed *something*.

My head turned as she walked into the room. And my heart slammed against my ribcage.

A vision of perfection, a stunning enchantress stealing my breath, my thoughts, corrupting logic, self-control, and numbing everything in my body except for the blood funneling between my legs.

Temptation.

Desire.

Risk.

A flawless white against shimmering silk that draped her body like black gold, the fabric creasing enough to display her erect nipples. Like a magical nymph, her hair, dear God, an endless river of blonde, loose braids weaving down the sides, begging me to untangle them. Her lips, a soft red, plump and pouty, just below the red-hot flame behind those blue eyes.

Yeah, I needed something.

I needed *her*.

~

Erika

The look in his eyes had me taking a step back. A sudden combination of fear, excitement, desire, that my brain deciphering as a threat, while my body ignited from the inside out.

He stepped forward, closing those few inches between us and cupped my face in his hands.

My heart thudded as if my body knew what was about to come next, a thunder in my ears so loud it was as if all other senses had been removed.

His jaw twitched as he looked down at me, his lips

pressed in a thin line as if he were fighting a battle in his head.

A battle he lost.

Axel Steele leaned down and kissed me.

A slow simmering kiss that had my heart stopping and knees weakening. His hand slinked through my hair to the back of my head as he explored my mouth with his tongue, dizzying me, pulling me into some sort of dream-like state where the only thing that registered were the sensations waving over my body.

I gripped the back of his wet T-shirt, more or less to steady myself, anchoring myself into place.

After an endless minute, he pulled away, chest rising and falling heavily, and looked into my eyes. Thunder boomed, a flash of lightning from outside reflecting in dark eyes with one thing in mind.

One thing I wanted more than anything in the world right then. And I was going to do whatever I needed to do to get it.

I lifted his shirt, and he ripped it off.

I gasped. Not because of the super-hero chest, or the scar down the ripples of a six-pack. But because of the small, whittled stone he had on a chain next to his dog tags.

My jaw dropped as I gaped up at him. "My stone."

He nodded. "Hope."

I breathed out... and fell in love with him. Right there in Cabin 2, I fell in love with Axel Steele.

The man I'd dubbed as having a sensitivity chip missing had taken my gift, something that meant so much to me, and placed it next to his heart.

Yeah, I fell in love with him.

He cupped my face again, kissed me again, devouring

me. Letting go. He smelled like fresh soap and rain, a scent that had every sensor in my body jumping to alert.

My *God,* I wanted him.

I wanted this man in every—*any*—way I could have him. I wanted to please him, the way he'd just pleased me.

My fingers ran down his back, shifted to his stomach as I slowly dropped to my knees, licking a trail down his abs. I stared up at him as I undid his belt, his button and zipper, and finally pulled down his pants.

Then, his boxer briefs.

I cupped his ass, my body turning to water as I gawked at Axel Steele, in all his magnificent, shocking glory.

As if I expected any less.

He stared at me with narrowed eyes, the fire dancing across his face, all alpha, all challenge.

I was up for this challenge.

I took him with my mouth, savoring the feel, the taste of him. My eyes drifted up to meet his, watching me, the fight lessening from his eyes as he melted into me.

"God, you're beautiful, Erika."

His hands threaded my hair as he closed his eyes and tilted his head back, inhaling as if he'd just injected the world's finest drug. I let him guide me, moving my head, a firm yet gentle grip reminding me that although he filled every inch of my mouth, he was still in control.

Sexy as hell.

A groan escaped his lips and he pulled my head back, then dropped to his knees.

The dress was pulled from my body, the silk tickling my skin as it was swept away. I lowered to a seated position, my legs tucked under me. He pulled back, admiring my bare, naked body, lingering on my breasts, then dropping to my stomach.

"Floor," he demanded, his voice low, husky, his eyes now wild with passion.

The fire crackled and hissed next to us as I lowered onto the thick Navajo rug, warmed by the flames. I watched him as he kicked off his boots and remaining clothes, then he grabbed two pillows from the couch. One for my head, and the other, he slid underneath my butt.

And then, without preamble, he spread my legs and returned my favor. With vigor.

My breath caught as his mouth slid over me, devouring the wetness I'd already become. He licked slowly at first, his tongue sliding between my inner folds, then pressed in while his hands trailed my thighs, my stomach.

A shiver ran over my skin and I opened wider, my body wanting to press into the sensation as much as possible.

Little did I know what was yet to come.

At the moment he had me thinking I was going to peak, the tip of his tongue found my clit, a light circling that sent a zing of electricity through my body. I writhed under him as he worked the tiny, swollen bud with a buildup sending me into a crazed fury of desire. Want.

Need.

Panting, I gripped his hair, pulled. "Come here."

He licked harder.

"*Now.* I have to have you," my voice, my plea, as desperate as I felt inside. "Please, Axel..."

His head lifted at his name rolling off my tongue.

The fire colored his skin as he moved over me, all man, all beast, shadowing my body. His lips found mine, his tip my opening, and with a thrust only Ax could deliver, he slid into me, every inch inciting a heatwave of tingles through my insides. I couldn't take it, so I did. My face squeezed as he pressed into me, deeper, hitting places I'd never felt before.

"Are you okay?" He whispered in my ear.

"Yes." I gripped his back, my nails digging into his skin, the sweet tinge of pain reminding me—no, screaming at me—how powerful he was. What a *man* he was.

I couldn't take it, and I loved it.

"Ax. *Take me.*"

He crushed his lips onto mine, his hand sliding to the back of my head, cupping. Each thrust hitting deeper, deeper inside me.

I pulled away from his lips, because I needed to breathe. It was as if my body was not my own, it was his.

My body was his.

I tilted my chin up and arched my back as he drove into me, begging for more. We fell into a rhythm, a perfect wave of euphoria, building, building together.

A quiver ran between my legs, the friction against my clit increasing with each thrust. His breath picked up, a sheen of sweat coating his skin.

My body squeezed around him, inexplicable tears filling my eyes.

"Fuck, *Erika,*" his husky voice breathed in my ear.

"Oh, Ax," I whimpered out, my voice shaky, desperate.

"Say it again," he pleaded.

"Ax, oh, Ax. Shit, *Ax.*"

My body exploded from the inside out, sparks blurring my vision as the orgasm ripped through me, his warm wetness filling me at the same time.

Panting, we collapsed together, Ax wrapping me in his arms, so tightly, as if he didn't want to let go.

To let me go.

We laid in silence, with only the distant thunder and crackling fire at our side, his grip on me never wavering.

I turned my face to his, met a pair of dark eyes that I wasn't sure how long had been watching me.

We stared at each other, both knowing that what just happened changed everything. Both finally submitting to it. Two hot messes that had somehow found their anchors.

20

AXEL

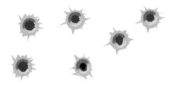

I stroked her cheek, gently, so not to wake her. A darkened room with only a dim nightlight shining from the bathroom couldn't even hide that beauty. Her little angel face, her long blonde hair fanned out over the pillow like silk.

My stomach knotted, looking down at her.

A foreboding of something to come.

A desperation to keep her close.

Because I knew in my heart, this woman had one priority, one single goal she wanted to accomplish, and that one thing could get her killed quicker than she could blink those endless lashes.

And the craziest part about it all was that she knew this. Erika knew the risks. But in her twisted psyche, it was revenge for her Baba.

And goddammit if I didn't understand that.

I understood hate.

I understood blinding vengeance and the crippling hold it had on you.

I didn't want *her* to understand it.

How could I take that away from her? Could I take the weight of the guilt she carried? How could I convince her that her grandmother wouldn't want her to pick up the sword?

How could I convince myself anymore that my feelings for her, the gut-wrenching, down in my soul, feelings for this woman were nothing more than a physical attraction?

Which would she choose, I wondered?

Me, or revenge for Baba?

Would *we* make it through this, I wondered?

My father had been taken from me, my brother barely breathing, and now a woman... a woman who'd entered my life and shaken me to my very core.

And that woman was a walking loose cannon.

The hunted... and the hunting.

I watched her breathe, a calm, smooth rhythm that I wanted to capture, to bottle, to give her every time she felt anxious. Every time she couldn't let the past go.

Because I couldn't bear to lose this one.

Not on my fucking life.

My phone vibrated on the nightstand. I rolled over and clicked it on—5:44am—and read the message.

Damn, dammit, dammit, *dammit.*

After checking on Erika one more time, I pushed out of bed, pulled on my clothes and stepped out the front door.

"Morning," I said to the movement behind me as I slid the locks into place and keyed in the code.

A grunt in response.

I stepped off the deck. Dawn was yet to break, and thanks to the lingering clouds, the morning was still black as night. Bugs screamed around us as we took a few steps away from Cabin 2.

"Did you come straight from the hospital?" I asked.

"Yep. Relieved Gage around midnight." Gunner looked blankly at the cabin, the exhaustion and stress draining his face.

"How is he?"

"Same."

"Alright. I'm going to head that way. Who's on next?"

"You're six to ten, Gage is ten to two, and I'm back on after that."

"Dallas there?"

"Stopped by thirty minutes ago. Brought muffins and coffee... although Big-bootied-Brianna just started her shift..."

"So you're saying I need to pick up some more on the way in."

"I'll do it. I'm going to swing back by after I'm done here."

I tilted my head. "You got the hots for Booty-B?"

"You know I love a good set of curves, but..." he frowned, shook his head.

"I know... I know."

A moment passed, the strain of the last few weeks settling around us like cement. Darkness had swallowed my older brother and no amount of light, or booty for that matter, was going to break the six-inch safe he'd closed himself into. I'd say I understood, but that all changed overnight when Erika had broken through mine.

And wasn't that something.

I caught Gunner looking at me with a cocked brow. "How's she?" He nodded to the cabin.

I glanced down and nodded, telling him everything without a single word.

"Feen wouldn't approve, you know. She's a client."

"Yes he would," I replied quickly, and meant it. Feen would want me to be happy.

"Alright, bro, just keep your head on straight, okay?"

"You don't have to worry about that. I'm not Gage."

Gunner chuckled, then focused again on the cabin. "Okay, so recap me again—I'm supposed to let you know if this chick sets foot outside of her cabin, right?"

"Erika. Her name is—"

"Oh my *God*—"

"Yes. And you're supposed to call me, but to follow her if she leaves. Make sure she doesn't get herself into any shit."

"Until you get back?"

"Yep."

He glanced at his watch. "No problem."

"Thanks. I'll have a six-pack and football on for you in the den after. And Booty-B if you're lucky."

He snorted.

"See ya, bro."

Gunner called out for me as I walked away.

"Yeah?" I turned.

"He's a little paler, Ax." His voice cracked. If not for growing up with him, I wouldn't have even noticed. "Just FYI."

I swallowed the knot in my throat and nodded, then slipped into the woods.

21

ERIKA

"*If* you're going to be hanging around outside my cabin all day, you might as well get a workout in." I grinned.

Leaning against a tree, Gunner's eyes never left the gun he had dismantled in his lap. "If you think you snuck up on me, you might as well deliver yourself to the Black V's."

"Oh come on, you didn't even flinch. Admit it, I got the drop on you."

He methodically began reassembling his gun with the speed and efficiency of someone who'd done it a million times, and for some reason, I had no doubt that he had.

Without looking up, he said, "You woke up at seven twenty-three, meandered around the cabin for a bit—I'll pretend I don't know you were looking for Ax—before staring out the back window for so long I had to make sure you weren't having some sort of episode. Then, you made some coffee, and if I had to guess, inside the small, white mug you'd chosen was just as much sugar as the tar you made. Who puts four scoops in for one cup? Then, you painted for a bit—impressive, that I will admit. Next up, a shower. Based on the amount of steam, I'd say piping hot—"

I cocked a brow and crossed my arms over my chest.

"Don't worry, I didn't see anything, much to my dismay. After that, more painting. But then you became restless. So, now, here you are in a pair of camo leggings, grey tank top with a small tear in the left bottom corner, underneath a blue jogging jacket, an orange scrunchie in your hair—that Celeste would have a field-day with—about to ask me if I would like to go on this jog with you. Not because you want me to, but because you know if I'm anything like my brother that you've fallen madly in love with, you know that I'd take a bullet before letting you out of my sight, because of the commitment I made to my younger brother."

With a click, the last piece of the gun slid into place. Gunner pushed off the ground and finally faced me, gun in hand. My chin came up, noticing he was a few inches taller than his over-six-foot brother. When I'd met Gunner for the first time at the main house, he'd stayed in the shadows, more or less, observing the interaction between my brother and his brothers. The term, a 'silent professional' came to mind. The man had an undeniable presence. Like Ax, he was built like an ox and had that ruggedly handsome thing to him. He resembled his twin brothers, but with less quar- terback-of-the-football-team swagger to him. There was something different with Gunner, something darker, less poster-boy. Something ice-cold behind eyes as black as coal that, quite honestly, sent a chill up my spine.

Towering over me in an intimidating way that was either intentional or part of the brash demeanor that was Gunner Steele, he said, "So, Erika Zajac, you tell me if I knew you were sneaking up behind me like a six-hundred pound gorilla."

My mouth opened to respond, but I wasn't quite sure how to address the hostility looming over me. I was considering slinking back inside, when he said—

"Take off that jacket."

"What? It's fifty something degrees out here."

"Fifty-seven to be exact. And you're going to regret it when we start climbing the mountain. I'm not carrying it for you."

I zipped it up, another childish display of defiance that I was starting to get sick of myself. "I'm good," I said.

"Suit yourself. Let's go." He shoved the gun in the band of his pants and took off.

"Wait."

He stopped, blew out an annoyed breath as he turned.

"You're in jeans and boots. I can wait while you change."

"Why would I need to change?"

"... ... Alrighty then." *Geez.*

We took off in a jog, slow at first and then building speed, like a dial that was slowly turning up. I realized he was pushing me, testing me, seeing how fast I would tire out and wave the white flag. He knew that each of his strides were double my own, but he didn't care. He was challenging me, maybe because he didn't like me, or because of my relationship with his younger brother—which he'd obviously picked up on.

We were in a full sprint by the time we started ascending the mountain. I was drenched with sweat under that damn jacket.

I looked over at Gunner, barely even breathing heavily.

I grit my teeth and pressed harder, leaping over a fallen log and pulling ahead of him.

And that was pretty much how our hour-long jog

through the woods went—me being inches from catching up, and then him pressing faster.

Bastard.

My legs were numb by the time we'd made it back to Cabin 2. Gasping for breath, I braced myself on the railing.

Gunner resumed his place in the shadows.

"Thanks for the jog," I said, half sarcastic, half serious. I turned and met a pair of narrowed, black eyes. A single bead of sweat rolled down his face.

"Axel doesn't need any more drama in his life right now."

I tipped my chin up. "I understand."

"Do you?

"Yes."

He stared at me for a moment, then turned and disappeared back into the woods.

"You don't have to spy on me, you know. I'm not going anywhere." Watching him from the corner of my eye, I pushed through the front door.

He didn't believe that any more than I did.

Dense clouds had moved in, keeping the temperatures low and the sun out. It was a dark, dreary afternoon, the wind scented with a hint of rain. My stomach was in knots, my heartbeat never quite evening out after my run.

It was time.

Gunner was right, Ax didn't need any more drama. And frankly, I didn't either. Things needed to be done, to be taken care of.

Things needed to be ended.

So I waited, painting, watching the tree line outside until finally, Ax appeared through the shadows and dismissed his brother from my watch. Our eyes caught through the window, my heart skipping a beat. The corner of his lip curled up, then he shifted his attention back to his brother, before joining him in deep conversation as they disappeared down the pebbled path that led to the main house.

No, Ax didn't need any more stress in his life. He didn't need me.

After waiting a good twenty minutes after that, I packed up my easel, canvas, and paints, and took one last look at the view from my cabin.

He was out there. I could feel him.

And it was time.

I turned from the windows, catching a glimpse of myself in the bedroom mirror.

For you, Baba.

Gritting my teeth, I slid out the back door, scanning the woods to ensure I was alone. A gust of wind swept past me as I slipped into the woods, dark with impending rain. My heart started to pound with each step, not knowing what was going to happen. The only thing I knew was that I, and I alone, was the means to an end. He wouldn't stop hunting me, Ax knew it as much as I did. And, as he'd done for thirteen years, he'd evade the cops, hiding out in whatever hole in the ground he lived in. Or, behind whatever identity he'd created for himself.

It was time to face him, face the nightmare that had never let me go.

As my grandma would say, *Que Sera Sera.*

What will be will be.

You probably think I was verging on a panic attack as I journeyed deeper into the woods, dangling myself like bait, wondering what it was like to be walking to your death.

Let me tell you.

It was a shot of adrenaline, the culmination of a life filled with fear, guilt, regret, and anger, finally coming to its head. To say I was ready was an understatement. Hell, it was almost as if I were excited. Finally, the day was here. The end.

Que Sera Sera.

My pace quickened with my pulse as I walked down the very path Ax had led me down the day before. Finally, I spotted it. The old oak tree standing firm among a tornado of swirling leaves. Taking a deep breath, I maneuvered though the brush and began setting up my easel.

A single beam of sunlight shot through the clouds, sparkling against the golden leaves against the tree. I could almost see Ax with his older brother in that tree. Back when times were easy, happy. Good.

With a smile, I settled in and began painting. It would be my gift to him, to Ax, to the man I'd fallen in love with. Whatever happened, this would be my gift to him.

I dipped the brush in the paint and began painting the tree.

A tear rolled down my cheek, with one stroke after another, emotions that could never be portrayed in any other way than through colors. He would get it.

Ax would understand.

He would love it.

I painted, and painted, and painted.

And I waited.

22

AXEL

J watched her, her long blonde hair blowing in the breeze as she somehow captured a memory with each stroke of her brush, my brother and I, right there on her canvas.

I loved her.

Dear God, and everything Holy in the world, I loved that woman.

From my spot hidden behind a thicket of bushes, I was transfixed, hypnotized, watching her paint, the memories unfolding in front of me.

I was going to be with Erika Zajac for the rest of my life. She was mine, I was hers, it was written in the stars.

But, in step with the last year, that moment of pure happiness, peace, love, was shattered by the sound of a twig breaking behind me.

I didn't think things could get worse.

They did.

Every sensor in my body shot to alert, every instinct informing me of danger. Someone else was in the woods.

A gust of wind whipped past sending the leaves around

me into a swirl of white noise, blocking my attempt to zero-in on movement around me.

Around Erika.

He was here. He'd come.

And he wasn't making it out of these mountains alive.

Adrenaline pulsed through me as my eyes darted to Erika, unaware of whatever was hunting her, then back to the woods around me.

And then I saw him. The tall, fat bastard with his bald head and tattooed skin.

Rent-a-guard was crouched behind a bush, his focus locked on his prey—the newly-discovered love of my life.

Mack, the fucking bodyguard. I should've known.

Rage gripped me, so tight that it felt like my lungs were going to collapse on top of each other. They say when you're protective of something, you shield it, care for it, set it up so that nothing bad ever happens to it. When you're possessive about something, you want it only as your own.

I was both protective and possessive of Erika.

Erika was *mine*. Mine to protect, mine to have. Both emotions inciting a firestorm of fury in me so hot that my thoughts, my rationale, my common sense dissolved into a singularly-focused goal to kill the man who wanted to take her from me.

I pulled the gun from my belt and set off through the woods with the stealth of a lion hunting its prey. The difference? A lion was patient, cool-headed. I was a sizzling fuse about to explode.

Savage. Feral.

Lethal.

I cut through the trees and came up behind him, my heartbeat a hammer in my ears. Closer, closer, until I was less than three feet from him. He didn't even hear me. His eyes were trained on Erika, painting in the short distance.

Gun lifted, my finger slid over the trigger.

Mack burst through the bush with his own gun—pointed at Erika's head. I lunged forward, knocking the gun from his hand. We tumbled to the ground, rolling down the hill and landing with a *thud* against a boulder.

I'll admit the boy had a bigger fight in him than I'd anticipated. He caught me with a right hook, answered back by an uppercut and kidney shot. He liked that. Blood pooled in my mouth as we squared off in a solid match of hand to hand combat, neither of us knowing where the hell our guns had flown to. I lunged first, of course, knocking him onto his back. We wrestled, fists flying. I had gravity to my advantage, pulling the fat bastard's body to the ground as I pinned him, and noticed the black *V* tattooed on his upper arm. He took advantage of that spilt-second of wavering attention and rolled on top of me. The son of a bitch wrapped his hands around my neck. I'd been choked out before, mainly by my brothers, but never by a man that knew if *I* didn't die, *he* was going to die. I pounded the side of his face, his ears, jaw, but he squeezed, desperation and adrenaline fueling the strength of his grip. *Shit,* was my single thought before my vision started to waver. The grunts, shuffling of my legs, the sounds of nature around me beginning to fade in a *whomp, whomp, whomp* like helo blades cutting through the air. My fingers began to tingle, my strength flailing.

Erika.

Erika.

My heart skittered like a meth addict overdosing and my eyes popped open, the will to live sending one last spurt of adrenaline through my veins. I ripped his hands from my throat, and yanked him down to me as I sent my forehead into his nose. Blood spurted like a fountain raining over us. His eyes rolled back into his head as his body rolled off me. I spat out the blood from my mouth, gripped his head and bashed it against the flat rock.

Game over.

Using the cuffs from his own belt, I secured his limp body to a tree and sprinted to Erika.

And my heart stopped beating.

Erika was gone.

23

AXEL

J sprinted through the brush, my eyes darting the landscape as I neared the tree. My mind raced, my heart thundering in my chest. Someone took her.

There were two players. Mack had been nothing but a distraction, while someone else took her.

Son of a *bitch.*

Erika's easel had been knocked on its side, paint smeared over her beautiful creation. Leaves scattered under spilled paint. Her security necklace had been ripped from her neck.

She struggled, fought him.

My girl had fought him.

I frantically looked around, terror speeding through my veins clouding my ability to form a single thought, a single plan.

I was out-of-my-fucking-mind terrified.

Track, I thought.

Track her.

Track *them.*

Her face flashed through my head, those blue eyes, that

fire that lived inside her. She'd fought, for her grandma, for herself. For me.

But he hadn't killed her, I realized as my brain began to work again. He'd taken her.

Of course he had. The bastard had probably been ordered to take her to the Black V's, to redeem himself, earning their grace and his ability to continue to live. And if the past were any indication of the future, the Black V's would torture her before they killed her.

A video that would go viral within hours.

My gaze shifted to a break in the leaves, then another, then, another. I followed, tracking them deeper into the woods where the terrain became more rocky—where I'd lost the trail.

"Fuck," I spat out, turning in a circle.

And that's when I saw him.

Cassi, my thirty-six point white-tail, staring at me underneath a grouping of pine trees.

I stared back, frozen except for some sort of message forming in my head. A communication between me and the beast. Like a magnet, my leg moved forward, then the next, then the next, my eyes never leaving Cassiopeia. I moved through the brush, locked on his gaze, closer, closer.

I got within six feet of the buck I'd hunted for months. He was magnificent. I stopped, and the world did too, as we stared at each other. He dipped his chin, then turned and leapt through the forest, disappearing into the shadows.

I ducked into the pine trees where he'd been standing... and understood why I didn't pull the trigger that day.

Karma—A person's actions defining their future.

I spotted a flash of beige in the distance, a *you're welcome* through the trees, before I looked back down at the small ball of tobacco, glazed over with fresh saliva.

My Cassi had led me to him.

I grabbed my cell phone.

"Wolf here."

"Wolf, I need you to pull the security footage from the Fall Harvest Party. *Now.*"

"Dude, what's—"

"Now," I yelled.

Mad shuffling through the phone confirmed Wolf picked up on the urgency in my voice. A door opening, a few clicks, then, "Okay, I'll go as fast as I can but it will take me a second to hack into the hotel's cameras."

My heart was a jackhammer as I waited, knowing each second was pulling Erika further and further away.

"Wow, they really need to upgrade. I'm in."

I began pacing. "There's a guy—I'm guessing mid-forties —solo, horned gold mask, dark hair in a pony tail, vintage suit, wad of tobacco in his mouth, so he's probably carrying a Styrofoam cup. Find him."

I took off in a sprint toward the main house, unable to stand still a minute longer. The seconds I waited for Wolf to scan the footage felt like hours, days, years.

"Got him. Caucasian, about five-eleven."

"That's him. I need a name."

"Hmm..."

"There was a sign-in sheet at the entrance. See if you can zoom in when he comes in."

"Good thinking... hang on... alright, there he is. Let me zoom in on the book... Annnnd... your tobacco-sucking boy is named Lex Moreno."

"Lex Moreno," the name rolled off my tongue like venom. "That's him. That's our guy, Wolf. That's our guy."

"You mean the cellar gangster?"

"Yep."

"Holy shit."

"I need his location right now. He's got Erika."

"Okay, it will take a bit to pin down his cell phone but I can get you his home address fairly quickly."

"No. No, he wouldn't take her to his house, no way. He'd take her directly to the Black V's. Every second matters to him. No..." My hand clenched to a fist as my mind reeled. "They'd make him meet at an alternative location. *Shit...* does he have any other addresses?"

"No. No, man, I'm not seeing anything."

My heart raced picturing Lex Moreno in my head, the cocky swagger, the way he'd kept looking at Erika. The minutes between seeing him and the shots ringing out. He hadn't meant to kill her that night, no, he'd meant to create a diversion and take her. I pictured the music, the dancing, our conversation about his suit—vintage, classic... ...

"Wait. There was a classic car there. A 1959 Cadillac Eldorado. Where would someone get a car like that around here?" I burst through the woods and sprinted to the garage.

"Without question, a vintage car shop on the outskirts of town. Been there a few times. You think...?"

"Yeah, bring it up."

"Hang on... *Whoa,* guess who's on the cover of the webpage? Lex Moreno owns it."

"Text me the address."

"Done."

"Okay, I need you to call the cops, tell them Lex Moreno is a member of the Black V's and killed Jessa Watson. Tell them he's got Erika and to send all available units to the shop. Got it?"

"Got it."

I jumped on my Harley. "Tell Gage to get his ass down to the tree Feen and I used to climb when we were kids. He'll know the one. There's a guy cuffed to a tree nearby. I need him to stay with him until the cops can take care of him. Also, about thirty feet southwest of that, in a thicket of pine trees, is a ball of tobacco. Tell the police to bag it up—that's our guy's DNA to prove he was at the scene. And send Gunner to the car shop. I have a feeling I'm going to need backup."

"Anything else?"

"Yeah..." the knot in my throat tightened. "There's a painting, um, in front of the tree Feen and I used to climb... can you take it somewhere safe? I don't want anything to happen to it."

"Yes, I'll handle it personally."

"Thanks, man."

"Ax, you okay?"

I started the Harley, the growl echoing through the woods like a warning.

"I don't know yet."

I disconnected the call, memorized the directions and sped down the driveway praying I'd make it on time.

Erika

"Get out."

The car door opened and I was pulled out by my hair, stumbling to my knees. Pain rocketed through my side as a boot slammed into me.

"Get up."

I ground my teeth, tasting the blood from when he'd punched me in the face when I tried to escape. After he'd tied my hands behind my back it was no use. I pushed to my feet, pain vibrating through my body, wave after wave, making my stomach curdle and my hatred for him peak.

He'd snuck up behind me in the woods, the only indication of his presence was the cool blade that had appeared at my jugular. He'd forced me to stand, the blade piercing my skin when I'd hesitated, replaying every second of Ax's self-defense lesson. Pulling from that, I elbowed the bastard in the gut and sent my heel into his shin, then lunged forward. And I'll be damned, it worked. But I got about twenty feet before stumbling on a root. He caught me, punched me with a force like a sledge hammer, then bound my wrists before pressing the knife at my neck again and forcing me through the woods. But I'd seen his face before his fist pummeled my eye.

The horned gold mask, black ponytail, vintage suit, who I'd caught looking at me a few times at the Harvest Party. My instincts had piqued the moment I'd seen him.

Didn't help me much now.

The dreary afternoon had grown dark as twilight, as if it knew of the darkness unfolding. I'd been taken to an old, rusted metal building deep in the woods. Snarled roots of dying shrubs lined the sides, the long, crooked branches of an old maple tree encasing the building like witches' fingers.

One of the two garage doors began to open.

The clouds above broke, sprinkles raining down on me as I watched in horror at what was about to come out of that garage.

Flanked by two massive security guards, a man wearing a blue pinstripe suit stepped out of the shadows, his dark, narrowed eyes scanning my body from head to toe.

Senator Inglewood.

I was thrown to the ground, my cheek slamming into the

cold, wet dirt. The senator stepped over, shiny black wingtips at my nose.

"Looks like she put up a fight, Lex," his deep voice was calm and absolutely chilling.

Lex.

"Naw, she's nothing but a weak bitch."

The rain picked up, the sprinkles turning into a deluge at my back. I raised my head, blinking the water from my face. At least a dozen more men had slinked out of the garage, several behind the senator, the rest stationed at each corner of the building, as well as the entrance of the driveway. Each holding AK-47's.

I was trapped, surrounded.

But I didn't give up.

"I have money," I forced out as strong and confident as I could, even though my insides felt like water.

The Boss, aka Inglewood, snorted, glanced down at me with a tilted head. "Does it look like I need money?"

"Maybe not you personally, but your operation does."

"And what do you know about my operation?"

A slow tingle, like sparks from a fire swirled in my stomach, a rage I'd never felt before in my life. I gritted my teeth and stood up. I turned away from Inglewood and turned, face to face, with Lex. Guns raised to my head as the rain poured onto me.

I took a step forward.

A gun pressed into the nape of my skull.

"I know that the forty-six dollars and sixteen cents you stole off my grandma after beating her to death was probably enough to buy those cheap-ass plugs you call hair." I spat in his eye.

A pistol whipped the side of my face, followed by kicks to my body that felt like cannon balls blasting my sides.

That was the first moment I felt real fear.

The pain, the cracking of bone, the sound of their grunts as they beat me.

A knock in the head sent my world spinning and an image of my grandma materializing in my brain—the image of her telling me that she was proud of me. Tears mixed with the rain sliding down my face as I faded in and out of consciousness.

I'm coming, Baba.

I'm coming.

"Stop." The single word from Inglewood's mouth registered through my haze. The world around me went still. I looked up. The dim light sparkled off the barrel of a pistol as he handed it to Lex.

My gaze flittered to the men circled around me, stopping on the one holding a cell phone camera.

I closed my eyes at the sound of the bullet sliding into the chamber.

I'm coming, Grandma.

24

AXEL

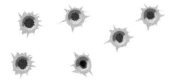

*Y*ou'd think my heart was pounding, the desperation and fear so overwhelming I wouldn't be able to function as I watched Lex Moreno beat the woman I'd fallen in love with. You'd think the panic would have been so paralyzing that I wouldn't have been able to hold myself back, as I slinked through the trees.

You'd be wrong.

In every mission there comes a moment where every bit of training, all the sleepless nights, every target hit, life taken, everything you learned comes together in one split-second when you need it the most. You don't pull from the playbook, you pull from your gut. That's the difference between a man and a soldier. You see, when there are no more options, when your back's against the wall, when all the fucking odds are against you, a switch flips. A switch that blurs the line between beast and human.

The will to live was strong, but the will to save something's life you put above your own? Takes it to a whole other level of savagery. Because at that moment, not a single thing in the world would have stopped me from saving my woman.

My breath was calm, my pulse a steady beat as I slid out of the tree line and climbed the red maple like a snake, slithering through the branches, higher, higher, higher. Even as I heard her grunts over the laughter of the guards, I stayed focused, edging myself down the longest branch, avoiding every fragile leaf, every twig, until I was directly above them.

My eyes narrowed with each man—nine to be exact—the corner of my lip curling. Nine men about to take their last breaths.

Nine against one.

I'll take those odds any fucking day of the week.

Adrenaline began to pick up, my body knowing shit was about to go down. Men were about to die.

A bloodbath in the rain.

My gun was somewhere on the forest floor next to Rent-a-guard's, so I pulled the KA-BAR from my boot, my fingers tingling as I gripped the hilt of the knife.

A gun was raised to Erika's head.

The world around me faded, the sounds, the rain, the beating of my heart as I edged farther down the tree limb, which was beginning to bend under my weight.

A bullet slid into the chamber.

That's when everything turned into a blur.

I released a guttural scream as I slid off the branch, raising the knife as I fell to the earth. I heard the pop of Lex's kidney before my feet even touched the ground. I pulled out my blade, blood dripping down my clothing as I heard the first gunshot.

Bullets exploded around us as I threw myself over Erika's body.

25

ERIKA

Forty-eight hours later...

My eyes drifted open, a blurry kaleidoscope of colors swirling in front of me. I blinked waiting for my brain to catch up as the room around me began to register. Ax's room.

A dim light shone in the corner, the smell of fresh coffee and burned incense lingered in the air. Movement on my hand had me turning my head.

"Good morning."

A smile spread over my lips, an automatic joy deep from within from simply seeing his face. I started to push myself up.

"Stop, baby, hang on." Ax jumped to his feet and began stacking pillows behind my back and guiding me up.

I squeezed my face at the lightning shooting through my torso. The grip on my hand tightened, along with every muscle in Ax's body.

"I'm okay." I fell back against the pillows and ran my finger over his palm, willing the fury behind those eyes to dissipate. It was the same look I'd seen on him every hour that I'd awoken to his face over the last two days. "I'm feeling better."

"Liar."

"Fine." I smiled.

He smiled. "You look good in my bedroom."

"You look good all the time.... What time is it?"

"One-forty-four," he replied instantly as if he'd been watching the clock tick. And he probably had been.

He pulled a tray from the top of the dresser and nestled it on my lap. A bowl of chicken soup, flaky French bread, and a tall glass of ice-water.

I cocked my head. "The soup is warm and ice isn't melted. How did you know when I was going to wake up?"

"I've been refreshing it every thirty minutes."

I shook my head. "Ax, you don't have to tend to me like this. You've got your job, a life. I'm fine, I promise, you—"

"You're my job, my life right now, Erika." He tucked a strand of hair behind my ear. Goosebumps followed his fingertip. "Can you eat? Will you eat?"

"I will, as soon as you tell me what I've missed."

As if on cue, the low buzz of an alert pulled our attention to the TV in the corner. "Breaking News," followed by an image of a cuffed Senator Inglewood being guided into the back of a cop car, followed by a line of men, each sporting black V's on their forearms.

I looked at Ax. "Tell me."

He began pacing next to the bed. "It's big, Erika. Huge. Seventeen arrests so far, and according to Jagg, a treasure trove of evidence linking the Black V's to dozens of murders and cold cases, and a trail leading the feds to almost all the members. It's a global operation. Senator Inglewood is the big fish, the leader. Guy's been in the game since he was a teenager. We got him. It's going down."

I closed my eyes and inhaled, then felt the mattress sink under Ax's weight as he sat beside me.

"And it's all because of you, Erika. You single handedly took down a global organization responsible for the murders of hundreds of people. Hell, maybe thousands over the decades."

I exhaled. A moment passed.

"Erika..." Ax grabbed my hand, the twinkle in his eyes sending a swirl of butterflies in my stomach. "You did it. Baba is proud."

Tears welled up.

"Erika..." He reached into his pocket and pulled out a small, red, velvet satchel.

My heart skipped a beat as our eyes met. Call it a gut instinct, call it my sixth-sense. Call it being in tune with the man who'd taken over your soul.

He handed the satchel to me, my hands unsteady as I pulled the tassels.

A small, gold ring with three blue stones tumbled onto my lap.

"My ring..." The words a breathy whisper. "Baba's blue-bird ring."

He nodded.

"How did you..." I turned it over in my hands. "Oh my God. Where did you..."

"A pawn shop."

"A *pawn* shop?"

"After the ring didn't turn up during the search at Lex's house, I went to a pawn shop on the outskirts of town that was rumored to be run by the Black V's. It was there."

"Oh my God."

"And I paid for it with hundred dollar bills currently being tracked by the feds. We'll get them all." He smiled.

I smiled. "Baba would like that. She'd like that very much." Tears released, uncontrollable emotions releasing in a river down my face.

Ax pulled me to him, stroking my hair, letting me cry.

"Thank you," I whispered.

"Marry me," he replied.

My eyes popped in disbelief. I pulled away and stared up at him. "Wha—

"I love you, Erika. I love everything about you. From your stubborn bullheadedness, to the raw *fight* you've got in you. The grit, the passion, the fire in your soul. My whole life I've analyzed, dissected, questioned, planned, thought out every decision I've ever made, but this? This?" Tears filled his eyes. "You, only you, have shown me something that is *un*questionable, undeniable, unbreakable. True love, a definite, finite thing like nothing I've ever been so sure of. *It* is, Erika. *It is.* I love you, my baby, and I want you by my side, forever."

He took the ring from my hand. "I want to marry you." A tear rolled down his cheek. "I want to marry you, Erika."

I grabbed his face, tears rolling down my cheeks.

And between kisses, I gave my heart, my soul to Axel Steele as he slipped my grandmother's memory onto my finger.

Erika Steele.

~

Two days later I was feeling exceptionally good, back to myself, the bruises beginning to fade.

The ring didn't hurt much, either.

"You ready?" I smiled as I slid my arm into Ax's—my new fiancé's.

"You're stunning." His gaze simmered over my body, the hunger making me want to pull him back to bed for round three.

Or was it four?

I gave him the once-over myself, in his black tuxedo and bowtie, the second sexiest thing I'd ever seen.

His naked body being the first.

I looked up at the banner that read, *Erika Zajac, Flight of the Bluebird Exhibit*. A ripple of butterflies fluttered through my stomach along with a rush of excitement.

I was myself. No more Agatha Rose.

Finally.

"Come on," I pulled him into the banquet room where more tuxedos and designer dresses drifted across the marble floor. Dozens of golden spotlights illuminating each one of my paintings that I'd donated to the cause.

Two causes, actually.

"Erika..." My brother stepped over, a bottle of beer in his hand.

"Whoa. No champagne?"

"Not tonight." Filip grinned, tipped it up. "Thank you for this. Your first painting has gone for six-figures."

Over the last two days I'd learned that my brother wasn't the businessman I'd thought he was, and had lead the family company into a mountain of debt. Harrison Reid had been the "secret CEO" for the last year, never leaving Filip's side, trying to pick up the pieces. And the reason Filip was so hellbent on sending me into hiding? It wasn't because he was afraid of losing more money, it was that he knew he'd have no way to pay the ransom in the first place.

I learned the sibling bond, even through the tough times, was one powerful force.

I tipped up my drink. "Only a few hundred more to get Zajac Investments out of debt."

He shook his head from side to side. "No..." A twinkle of pride caught his eyes. "I just sold the house. Yesterday."

"*What?*"

"Yep. Every penny is going into the business. I'm downsizing. I don't need dad's mansion. I'm fine in an apartment..." He held up his bottle. "Drinking cheap beer."

I couldn't hide my smile. "I'm proud of you."

"You inspired me. And I'll never be able to repay you."

"Let's start with being friends."

"You got it, sis."

Just then, a man with a short, grey crew-cut and blue suit stepped over.

"Ah," Filip said, "Erika, I'd like you to meet former Lieutenant Davis with the Marines."

"Axel." The man smiled fondly and stretched out his hand.

"Lieutenant Davis, long time no see."

They shook hands, then embraced, obvious acquaintances from a past life.

"I didn't realize you two knew each other," Filip looked back and forth between the two former soldiers.

"A past life."

"Indeed," Lieutenant David focused back to me. "Miss Zajac, I wanted to come here tonight to formally thank you for your kindness. Your generosity will help so many people who suffer daily."

I nodded and glanced down. I'd wanted to keep it a secret, although I wasn't sure why.

"Suffer?" Ax asked, head tilted.

"Ah, she didn't tell you? Your fiancée here is donating a portion of every sale to the PTSD Foundation of America. I know you understand the suffering and anxiety soldiers go through when they come home from war."

I felt Ax's gaze boring into me, my cheeks flushing.

"Erika…" His voice was low, deep.

Before I could look up, I was whisked into his arms, the public display of affection shocking me more than when he lifted me off my feet and planted a kiss on my lips.

A few whistles sounded across the room.

"I love you, Erika. You're the best decision I ever made."

"You're the only one I've ever made."

He smiled and kissed me again, and with that, the music started and the dancing began.

AXEL

I pushed through the cold door, my stomach doing its usual fade to water the moment I walked into my brother's hospital room.

Wolf glanced up from his laptop.

I nodded back, then glanced at Feen, the tubes coming out of his head, the machines beeping next to him.

The gray, waxy skin against almost iridescent lips. He started looking worse over the last few days, if that was even possible.

My brother.

My hero who'd I'd do nothing but stare at for the next four hours of my shift.

"Anything?" I asked.

Wolf shook his head and straightened from the pillow he'd been leaning against. "No, everything's the same. Four hours of nothing but male nurses and watching the local news about the gang bust."

"Male nurses, huh?" I grinned.

"Don't get too excited. They were asking for Dallas."

I laughed and Wolf blew out a breath. "Yep, not even a single woman to divert my attention."

"Lucky them."

"Damn straight."

I glanced out the window where twilight had settled in the mountains. "Passed Gunner on the way out."

"Headed to the range?"

"No doubt about that. Here." I handed him a box of pumpkin spice muffins.

"Dallas?"

"Yep. There's flax and some other healthy shit in there. Sugar free icing and gluten free."

"Mmmm." Wolf rolled his eyes and sat the box aside.

Just then, a rap at the door. Celeste dipped her head in, pausing.

"Come on in. There's muffins."

"Oooh, muffins." She made her way to the bakery box. "How's he doing?"

"Same. What're you up to?"

"On my way home, just thought I'd stop by. Check on everyone."

"How's Erika?"

Celeste smiled. "She's good. Dallas is making her something that involves kale."

"Dammit."

"I know. Don't worry, I snuck her a bag of Cheetos."

"Thanks."

She nodded to Wolf's computer. "What're you working on?"

He blew out a breath and focused on the screen. "It's seems like it's a safe bet that the Knight Fox lives here, in Berry Springs. And we believe The Fox killed that Russian dude, which started this whole mess."

"Right..." Celeste grabbed a muffin and hitched her hip onto the arm of the sofa.

He continued as she peered over his shoulder. "So, I'm thinking, why can't we pull all the names of people who traveled to Russia from here, around the time of Sokolov's murder?"

My brows popped up. "Not a bad idea."

"No, but..." Celeste said, chomping her muffin like a horse with a carrot. "There are four airports within driving distance. That's a lot of people to filter through, not to mention layers to hack through, even if you could."

Wolf held up a hand. "I don't know what I'm more pissed at, the crumbs you're dropping onto my four thousand dollar laptop, or the fact that you're questioning my hacking abilities."

She leaned back. "Sorry. Okay, what date range are we looking at?"

"Sokolov was murdered October twenty-fourth. So, really, I'd look at the month leading up, and after."

"It's a good lead," I said, my mind beginning to race. "I think it's something we should pursue. But there's also the private plane avenue to consider, too."

"Yeah, it's a lot but..." Wolf shrugged. "It's what I got."

"October twenty-fourth..." I repeated.

A muffin tumbled to the floor. "Oh. Sorry." Celeste dropped to her knees and began picking up the busted pieces.

I frowned, watching her suddenly jerky movements, her mind like it was running a mile a minute.

"What?" I asked her.

She blinked, looked up, licked her lips, then said, "What dates again?"

"October twenty-fourth, last year." Wolf said, kicking the crumbs away from his shoe.

"What is it, Celeste?"

"Nothing." She shook her head. "No, nothing. I just... was thinking about something else. Nothing." She stood and grabbed her purse from the sofa. "Anyway, good luck with all that. I've gotta head on out, boys."

I watched her scurry out of the hospital room, then turned to Wolf who was nibbling the rest of her muffin.

"What was that about?"

"Who knows. Probably that time of month."

"Gross."

"You know, these muffins aren't half bad."

"Take them all."

Wolf grabbed two in one hand, his laptop in the other, and stood. "Well, I'm out of here. I think Dallas has me back on shift tomorrow at noon."

"Alright man, enjoy your flax."

I watched him leave then turned my focus to my brother, where'd I stand for the next four hours.

It was almost midnight by the time Gage released me and settled in for his shift. It had been four hours of beeping machines and muted television, and racing thoughts of what I would do once I found the Knight Fox.

But one thing that kept interrupting those thoughts was Celeste, and what the hell her deal was all the of a sudden. I mean, Celeste rarely drops anything, especially food. Assuming the abrupt, odd behavior didn't have to do with her menstrual cycle—and let me tell you, Celeste was known for some rabid PMS outbursts—something was up.

And I wanted to know what it was.

So, after checking in with the house and confirming Erika was fast asleep in my bed, I made my way across town to Celeste's cottage at the base of Summit Mountain. I'll never forget when she purchased the place. The two bedroom, two bathroom house had been gutted, rotting from the inside out. But our tom-boy Celeste had seen something in it, and to our shock, turned it into a charming cottage lined with blooming flowers and bright shrubbery. She'd worked tirelessly alongside us and the local contractors to renovate it with her bare hands. It was quaint, feminine, and warm and welcoming—the polar opposite of Celeste.

And it made us all wonder if there was a side to her that she kept from us.

Like most women, we guessed.

I drove down the long driveway, my Harley a low growl through the silent night, and rolled to a stop next to the front porch. A dim light shone through pulled curtains—that was my first surprise. Celeste was up.

I cut the engine, something in my gut beginning to twist.

My gaze narrowed as I looked at the front door.

I'm not sure why, but I pulled my SIG from my belt as I slid off the bike. Celeste's Jeep was parked in her usual spot next to the house and from where I was standing, nothing seemed amiss.

I jogged up the steps and paused at the door, listening to every sound around me. The wind through the trees, the slow, tireless chirps of bugs.

Something wasn't right.

After a quick look over my shoulder, I tried the handle—unlocked.

Fuck, was my thought.

I turned the knob and with a double grip on my gun, I pushed the door with the toe of my boot.

"Celeste?" I called out, my pulse starting to pick up.

The faint scent of an Italian dinner hung in the air, the low chatter of the local news coming from a TV somewhere in the back. The air was still.

Heavy.

I stepped over the threshold, my foot sliding against the hardwood.

I looked down at the drops of blood speckling the dark floor. I shuffled, moving along the wall to avoid the droplets that faded into the house. Each room empty, each room quiet, undisturbed.

Until I made it to the living room—

Where a splatter of blood covered the walls.

~

Ready for Gunner's story?

From bestselling and multi-award-winning romantic suspense author Amanda McKinney comes book three in the steamy, edge-of-your-seat, three-part series, Steele Shadows Security…

Hidden deep in the remote mountains of Berry Springs is a private security firm where some go to escape, and others find exactly what they've been looking for.

Welcome to Cabin 1, Cabin 2, Cabin 3…

Businessman. CEO. Head of household. Three titles worst suited for Gunner Steele, the short tempered, reticent former Marine and rebel of the infamous Steele brothers. After an evening searching the mountains for his missing office manager, Gunner finds an undercover agent at his front door demanding protection—and that anyone *but him* be her bodyguard. Usually, Gunner didn't give a damn if someone disliked him, but this particular curvy vixen had information about the man who killed his father and maimed his brother. Information he'd gladly sell his soul for... but is he willing to sell hers, too?

After failure to deliver the location of a Russian spy as slippery as a bowl of borscht, Lexi York is fresh out of a job and a near-death experience when she seeks refuge at Steele Shadows, despite her disdain for the tattooed bad boy, Gunner Steele. At her wits end, Lexi devises a plan to use Gunner to get her job back, but what she hadn't planned on was developing feelings for the tortured soul she could never tame.

Unwilling to make promises he can't keep, Gunner is faced with the biggest decision of his life. Avenge his family, or throw away the only woman who's cracked open his shielded heart?

Grab your copy of *Cabin 3* today!

SNEAK PEEK

Cabin 3 (Steele Shadows Security)
Chapter 1

Lexi

My skin burned as the binds tightened against my wrists, the hard, wooden bench I'd been laid onto no longer cold underneath my heated back. Next, large hands grabbed my ankles and secured each to the slats at the ends. My eyes squeezed shut under the black blindfold they'd wrapped around my head, an almost involuntary reaction to the terror pumping through my veins. Every contact to my body, every touch, every sensation was amped up a million percent because I couldn't see it coming. My instinct was to try to see what was happening around me but I knew if I did, the last shred of control I had would be wiped away by total darkness. They'd taken my sight, my voice, my mobility, my freedom.

I swallowed deeply, the saliva like hot sand down my

throat. The sweet, metallic taste of blood seeped into my mouth from where the gag had rubbed me raw.

I inhaled through my nose. Then, exhaled, again and again, as I'd been trained to do.

Control your breathing, control your thoughts.

Control yourself.

I'd lost track of time, day, night, for every second I'd spent locked in a box no bigger than a dog cage, time had faded into some eternal black hole of neither past nor present. Just blackness.

It was the closest thing to hell I could imagine.

Just when I thought it couldn't get worse, the increased movement around me told me I was in for a rude awakening.

The room smelled old and dank. A musty scent that reminded me of the basement my sister and I used to escape and pretend we had a better life.

I zeroed in on the sounds around me. No words were spoken as my binds were checked. I'd counted two sets of boots against the concrete. One had gone still and I swear I could feel his gaze burning into me.

The one shuffling around me smelled of cigarette smoke and antiseptic, like a hospital, sending me into a horror show of scenarios that was about to happen to me.

I'd been scared before, but the fear I felt at that moment was so intense that I was sure to have a fatal heart attack if whatever these guys were about to do to me didn't kill me first.

My shoes and socks had been removed, leaving only the hospital gown they'd demanded I put on. I remember that moment vividly, the fear and panic that they were going to strip me naked. When they didn't, when they'd left the task to me, I remember being so grateful that I almost gleefully accepted being forced into a cage. They'd allowed me to keep my dignity. That "kindness" sent me into some sort of submissive state. It was a tactic, I knew that now. You've heard of Stockholm Syndrome where the victims fall in love with their captors? I could see now how that could happen. When you're in the depths of hell, with everything—including your freedom—stripped from you, something as simple as a toothbrush becomes the greatest gift in the world, momentarily replacing fear with genuine gratitude. I felt like because they'd let me keep my clothes, I owed them.

How totally screwed up is that?

Hospital-smelling guy walked away from me. A faucet turned on.

My insides turned to water.

Quite fitting.

His footsteps coming back were like a war drum through the silence, growing nearer and nearer, bringing me closer to whatever torture they were about to inflict. Then, nothing.

Silence.

A silence so unbearable, so terrifying, that in some uncontrollable reaction, I began fighting against my binds, thrashing on the bench they'd tied me to. I bit the gag, a guttural growl coming out of me. When the skin around my wrist tore open against the binds, I stopped.

Chest heaving, I laid there, gagged and blinded, my heart a steady thumping in my ears.

I jumped at the fingertips on my face. The gag was removed, and my jaw popped open, screaming every curse word I'd ever heard from the back alleys where I grew up.

Then, it happened.

A heavy piece of fabric was placed over my nose and

mouth. My entire body tensed in terror. Looking back, I actually smelled the water before it gushed over my face.

I know now why waterboarding was banned.

It is the most horrifying, indescribable mind warp that taps into a kind of panic that only few live to tell about.

When you think of torture, you probably think of pain. Let me take a second to introduce you to an entirely different kind of persecution. The kind that tortures the brain, not the body. There was very little pain involved with waterboarding. Instead, it triggered the deepest, most animalistic panic I'd ever experienced in my life. The sensation of drowning, suffocating, while being tied down has a way of breaking even the strongest-willed human. In a totally coherent state, you are gasping for air but getting none. Your lungs feeling like constricting brick walls about to cave in on each other. Every sensor piques, every voice telling you—no, *screaming* at you—that you are going to die. I felt like I was a witness to my own death. Dying, right there, dying on that bench. Totally aware of it happening to me.

You see with pain, your system releases endorphins, a natural pain and stress fighter, until eventually, you shut down. One way or another. Waterboarding is different. It is literally feeling like you are experiencing death while your mind and body are intact.

It was an experience that had haunted me every night, and every day, since.

The water stopped. The fabric was pulled away.

I spat, gagged, coughed, choking for air.

Then, again. The fabric, followed by more water, except this one lasted longer.

And this time, I vomited the moment the fabric was

removed. Water and bile spewing from the depths of my empty stomach.

Again, and again it happened, allowing just enough time between each assault for me to think it was over. Until finally, I felt my conscious begin to waver, a total submission to death.

I remember my body giving up, my mind giving up, an almost weightless sensation taking over, like I was floating up to heaven.

I was about to die. I'd given in.

"Enough."

The deep voice pulled me out of my dream-like state, like an angel granting me life. I recognized the voice instantly.

The wrap was removed from my eyes, a blinding florescent light sending a wave of nausea through me.

A large silhouette loomed over me.

"Nice work, Miss York."

"You sick, son of a—"

"Watch it. I'll take anything you've got as long as it doesn't involve my mother."

I twisted my neck to see the hospital-smelling man cutting my binds. I didn't recognize him.

The man only known as Astor, grabbed my hand and pulled me to a seated position on the bench. I looked around the room that had housed me for twenty four hours. The single light bulb above my head faded into dark corners with shelves, cages, chains, and rusty contraptions that rivaled any torture chamber. The walls were concrete, the floor, the ceiling, everything was a gray stone.

I jumped as hospital-guy reached for my wrists, his hands dry, cracked, with swollen knuckles and contorted thumbs. The guy looked like he'd seen his fair share of torture chambers.

"That's Davis," Astor said as the binds were cut. "He's the only one on payroll I've got that will do this."

I sent Hospital my most intimidating scowl—to which the corner of his lip turned up—then rubbed my wrists as I put my feet on the ground. I spat blood-tinged water, missing Astor's calf-skin Italian wing-tips by less than an inch. My aim was off.

"So." Astor casually began lowering the sleeves he'd rolled up to his elbows, as if he hadn't just ordered a woman to be tortured within an inch of her life. "That was water-boarding. A few more seconds and you would have experienced dry drowning, asphyxia, and let me tell you, that *does* hurt. Believe it or not, it could have been worse. Most victims who survive suffer damage to the lungs, permanent brain damage from lack of oxygen, and physical damage from the restraints. Not to mention the psychological damage. That reminds me..." He turned to Davis. "Call Mallory. Get an appointment set up for Miss York—"

"It's not necessary." I said.

"Yes, it is." With Astor, there was no way other than his own. He tossed me a towel and I began wiping down my face. "You did well. Are you ready for phase three of your training?"

I froze, peeking out from the towel. "Phase *three?* There's *more?*"

The wicked smirk on Astor's face had my gut clenching. At that moment, I considered running. Throwing in the proverbial towel. After all, what human would subject themselves to more?

It had been four weeks of what I can only assume was similar to special agent training at the FBI. For fourteen days, dawn until dusk, I was thrown into rigorous self-defense classes, hand-to-hand-combat and firearms training, and surveillance tactics. I was immersed in hours of foreign affair lectures worthy of a bachelor's degree. I'd lost ten pounds and had slept about the same amount in hours. Then, I'd entered phase two of training—escape and evade, otherwise known as SERE training. Little did I know this included the real-life scenario of being captured, ending with the blessed event of waterboarding.

At that point, most with half a brain would have tapped out.

Sayonara, you sick bastards.

But, you see, I was a different breed. I didn't tuck tail and run. Never had. Blame it on being raised by a single mother who was never there, or growing up in public housing in the Bronx. Whatever. I didn't care to psychoanalyze it.

The challenge had been laid down.

And I picked it up.

Astor turned and started across the basement—my cue to follow.

After sending Davis another glare—God, I hated him—I pulled on the robe I'd been tossed, and followed Astor up the rickety wooden steps. The heavy steel door opened up to a bland office hallway that gave no indication of the torture chamber below.

We rounded a corner where a group of polished twenty-somethings waited impatiently for the elevator on their cell phones. A cloud of over-priced French perfume lingered in the air, an announcement of their presence in the hallway. More like an air horn. The hot-rolled blonde, with a pitched voice that rivaled the music I'd been forced to listen to while in my cage, was demanding answers into her bejeweled cell phone about a late report. She was very important. The other, I'll call her Goldie Highlights, was texting into an oblivion, her fingers surely about to catch fire. My guess was that the texts had nothing to do with work and more to do with the Millennial she'd met at the bar the night before and how after agreeing to go home with him, she promptly retreated when things got "all too real." Both were one-hundred pounds of spin-class perfection, donning six-inch heels, designer suits and over-priced handbags. Both the living poster children for America's great entitled youth.

You should have seen their faces when I walked up.

I didn't need a mirror to tell me my eyes were as black as a raccoon's butt and as swollen as Davis's knuckles. My tangled, matted hair was sopping wet, the brown—*unhighlighted*—strings hanging over a dingy robe, loosely tied around my waist. No shoes topped off the lab rat look, complete with a disorientation in the form of unrelenting aggression.

I cocked my head and flashed a wide grin, knowing I had blood on my teeth. "Do you have any gum? I'm a little parched."

Astor groaned next to me.

Their perfectly lined eyes widened in horror, then, scanned me from head to toe in a way that took me back to the sixth-grade lunchroom. Then, with cocked brows, they dismissed me and refocused on their phones.

I didn't like being dismissed.

So I did what any temperamental toddler who'd just been waterboarded would do and slapped the phone out of Highlight's hand, sending it clamoring on the floor.

"Hey!"

The elevator dinged. I winked at my two new best friends, then followed Astor inside.

Fine, I was dragged in.

To no one's surprise, the girls waited on the next.

"I'm going to chock that up to low blood sugar, Miss York."

"I hope those aren't your next recruits."

"You'll have to work with all personalities as an agent with my company. If that's something you can't handle..." He pressed a button and the elevator screeched to a halt. The doors slid open. "There's the exit."

I took a silent deep breath reminding myself that this was the last stepping stone to my goal.

My life's goal.

"Miss York?"

"Proceed."

The doors slid closed and we were zipped up to the top floor where the sunlight from sweeping windows spilled into the hallway like warm butter. The city of New York gleamed below us, its glittering energy palpable even from fifty floors up.

I loved the city.

I was led down a hall that smelled like fresh flowers and into a corner office walled with windows. If God had an office, this was it.

And some people thought Astor was God.

"Food and water over there." He jerked his chin to the corner. "Eat."

My jaw dropped as I walked to the garden of Eden, a white linen-covered table topped with platters of fresh fruit, vegetables, shrimp cocktail, hummus, and just about every Keto-friendly food known to man. Ice-cold water and coffee completed the spread.

Coffee.

As I piled my plate, I skimmed the office, still cagey from "phase two." Astor checked emails behind his spotless, massive oak desk that sat next to a sculpture that I was sure cost a year's worth of my salary. Also, mildly inappropriate for an office setting.

Popping grapes like M&M's, I carried my loot to a seating area complete with brown leather sofas over a spotless Chinese rug.

Astor picked up a remote and a flat screen dropped down from the ceiling, in front of a walled bookshelf filled with leather-bound books that I had no doubt Astor had read cover to cover.

A grainy black and white surveillance image popped on the screen.

"Who's that?" I asked, a piece of shrimp flying out of my mouth onto the floor.

Astor pretended not to notice. "Sergei Orlov, aka, Bear."

I washed down the shrimp with a swig of coffee—FYI, a combination I don't recommend.

"Bear?"

"A nickname that he's almost exclusively known by. Bear was born and raised in the United States by a Russian immigrant and a white-collar heiress to a coal mining fortune. He grew up with a silver spoon in his mouth, and became quite the ladies' man as he got older. After inheriting his family's fortune, Bear started Eagle Technologies, a small tech company that exploded during the internet boom. Over the next decade, Bear doubled his net worth, as well as his ego." He clicked to an image of a bloodied man lying in an alley. "This is one of his associates." He switched to another image of a man lying in bed, his body beaten to a pulp, a bullet between his eyes. "And this is a childhood friend."

"Both murdered?"

"Yes. Both cold cases."

"And you suspect it's Bear."

"I don't. The US government does."

Another blurred image filled the screen with Bear and another man, flanked by two bodyguards holding AK 47's.

"That's Andrei Sokolov, a high ranking member of the Russian SVR—formerly the KGB—who was an advocate for stronger Russian-US relations. Sokolov was assassinated in his bed by a small group of Russians who we believe have embedded themselves into our society and are actively working for the Russian government."

"You're talking about spies? Foreign espionage?"

"Exactly."

"You said a small group? How many?"

"We're not sure. The information the government provided me was very limited."

I shoveled hummus into my mouth like a backhoe. "We know Bear's one of them?"

Astor turned, his six-foot-three presence towering over me. "That's what you're going to find out."

My eyebrows popped up. Surely I wasn't hearing him—

"Phase three of your training is to go undercover as an office assistant at his tech company and monitor his every move, providing me with actionable intel on a weekly basis."

With an audible gulp, the hummus slid down my throat like a bowling ball.

"Undercover?" I cleared my throat.

"That's right. Eagle Technologies is based in Dallas, Texas, where you'll reside as a former school teacher looking to start over after a nasty divorce with her husband."

I blinked.

"You will monitor Bear from a distance, get to know his colleagues and associates. Never get too close. Is that understood?"

I nodded, a million little incoherent questions racing through my brain.

Astor crossed his arms over his chest and stared down at me. "You're tough, Miss York. Your mother would have been proud. But I only hire the best. The success of my company depends on it. Which is why a full-time position with me depends on this last part of your training. If you succeed at bringing me actionable intel, phase three will be complete and we will discuss your future as an agent within my company."

Goosebumps prickled my arms. The end of the tunnel. The end of ten years of working tirelessly toward my goal of becoming a special agent with Astor Stone, Inc.

"I suggest you go home, recoup. Pack only what you need. You leave in forty-eight hours."

"Two days?"

"Is that a problem?"

"Uh. No sir."

"Good." He walked to his desk. "This should be a quick and painless assignment. Remember, your goal is only to *observe* Bear, nothing else."

I could do quick and painless... but something in my gut told me nothing about infiltrating a Russian espionage ring was going to be quick.

Or painless.

"You'll receive a visit from my assistant tomorrow where she'll provide you everything you need for your cover, including a detailed background story. You are to know it forward and backwards. You will no longer be Lexi York. You become your cover, understand? You are to remain unimpressionable, at best. People need to like you, then forget you the moment you walk away."

I'd like to think that part was going to be a challenge but

truth was, over the last few years, I'd become as boring as a dinner napkin. One of those plain white ones, not the delicate, ornate doilies. Lord knew there was nothing delicate about me. Despite my best efforts.

"Also, if you expect to be an agent with my company, you'll need to have that tattoo removed from your arm."

"My... But—"

"There's no but. It's as good as gone."

Shrimp in hand, I ran my knuckles over my arm.

His phone rang.

I decided to take an exit before he told me I had to cut off my hair. I grabbed my coffee and plate—because no way in hell I was leaving that goldmine—and stood.

"To be clear, Miss York. If you fail, you're out."

"Out?"

"Out of a job. You fail, therefore, you will no longer work at my company."

I blinked, my excitement dissolved by the pressure that just settled on my shoulders.

Then, it got heavier.

"I want to make it clear, Miss York, if your cover is blown, Astor Stone will deny having any knowledge of your visit to Texas. There will be no cavalry coming over the hill for you." He nodded to the exit—

"That'll be all."

～

ABOUT THE AUTHOR

Amanda McKinney is the bestselling and multi-award-winning author of more than twenty romantic suspense and mystery novels. Her book, Rattlesnake Road, was named one of *POPSUGAR's 12 Best Romance Books,* and was featured on the *Today Show.* The fifth book in her Steele Shadows series was recently nominated for the prestigious *Daphne du Maurier Award for Excellence in Mystery/Suspense.* Amanda's books have received over fifteen literary awards and nominations.

Text **AMANDABOOKS to 66866** to sign up for Amanda's

Newsletter and get the latest on new releases, promos, and freebies!

www.amandamckinneyauthor.com

If you enjoyed Cabin 2, please write a review!

Made in the USA
Columbia, SC
07 May 2024

35364846R00152